HIT LIST

HIT LIST

STUART WOODS

THORNDIKE PRESS
A part of Gale, a Cengage Company

GALE
A Cengage Company

Copyright © 2020 by Stuart Woods.
A Stone Barrington Novel.
Thorndike Press, a part of Gale, a Cengage Company.

LIBRARY OF CONGRESS CIP DATA ON FILE.
CATALOGUING IN PUBLICATION FOR THIS BOOK
IS AVAILABLE FROM THE LIBRARY OF CONGRESS

ISBN-13: 978-1-4328-7248-9 (hardcover alk. paper)

Published in 2020 by arrangement with G. P. Putnam's Sons, an imprint of Penguin Publishing Group, a division of Penguin Random House, LLC

Printed in Mexico
Print Number: 01   Print Year: 2020

HIT LIST

1

It was a list of names: ten of them; half men, half women.

John H. Williams
Sheila Barton
Randall Carver
Bethany Holmes
Ariana Charles
Mark Wiseman
Helena Tree
Richard Cianelli
Trisha Marshall
Stone Barrington

Neatly printed on heavy, pale yellow stationery. Stone Barrington didn't know any of them, except the last. He held it up to the light and found a watermark: *Strathmore.* He buzzed his secretary, Joan Robertson.

"Yeah, boss?" she asked, setting a cup of

coffee on his desk.

"There is a list of names on my desk. Who are they?"

"Beats me. I found it in the mail when I got to work — some time ago."

"Don't be arch, it doesn't suit you. Do you still have the envelope?"

She brought it to him; a plain, manila envelope, available at any store that sold plain manila envelopes. Not as distinctive as the stationery. He looked into the envelope and saw that it still had a card inside; he shook it out onto his desk. Same stationery, but card stock. One line, printed:

Dead, no special order, starting soon.
Figure it out.

"Is this one of your jokes?" Stone asked.

"What jokes? I don't have any jokes, just witticisms."

She had him there. "Did you see who delivered it?"

"No, it was already there when I arrived."

"Did you enter from the street?"

"No, I took the shortcut." Joan lived in the building next door, which housed Stone's staff.

"Joan, without touching either of these two pieces of paper, see if you can scan them and e-mail them to Dino." Dino Bacchetti had been his partner when they were detectives with the NYPD, many years before. Now Dino was the police commissioner for New York City, and Stone was an attorney at the firm of Woodman & Weld. In the beginning, he had handled the cases the firm did not wish to be seen handling; now he was a senior partner.

"Yes, sir." She left the room and came back in, pulling on a pair of latex gloves.

"You keep latex gloves in your office?" he asked.

"Yep. You never know when you might not want to touch something or leave any fingerprints." She picked up the two pieces of paper and left his office, closing the door behind her.

Stone had finished half his coffee when his cell phone rang. "Yes?"

"Is this some kind of joke?" Dino asked.

"I don't have any jokes, just witticisms," he replied, stealing a line.

"Tell me how you got them, and why, and no witticisms."

"A plain manila envelope was found by Joan when she came to work this morning. It contained both pieces of paper. There's a watermark on the letter paper: *Strathmore.*

9

It's common enough, but high quality. We use it here."

"Do you know any of the names on the list?"

"Only one: guess which."

"I'm familiar with two of them: yours and that of Randall Carver."

"Who is he?"

"He's an adman, director of account services at Young & Rubicam."

"How do you know, or know of, him?"

"The name is at the top of a form that landed on my desk about ten minutes before yours did."

"What form?"

"Homicide report. Carver's name is at the top. He was shot once in the head at the corner of Madison Avenue and Forty-second Street by a man on a bicycle, we think. A silencer was used; we found the bicycle around the corner, leaning against a dumpster. It was clean."

"You'll find my prints and Joan's on the paper, when you receive the originals; any others are fair game."

"You sure you don't know anybody on the list?"

"Only myself."

"My guess is whoever sent this killed Carver just to get our attention and start us working on the case. Now we have to figure out who all these people are, and that will be no picnic. The first name on the list is John Williams. I'll bet we can find two hundred of them in the phone book, if such a thing still exists."

"He has a middle initial, so it won't be too bad."

"Bad enough. It would have been nice if the killer had given us street addresses. Dinner tonight?"

"Why not."

"Viv is on the road, so it will just be me. P. J. Clarke's at seven?"

"Done." Stone hung up and buzzed Joan. "Please book me at P.J.'s for two at seven, then wrap up these two pieces and the envelope, while wearing your latex gloves."

"Consider it done."

"I will, when it's done."

After work, Stone went up to his fifth-floor master suite, to his dressing room. There were two — his and one for the putative woman. He opened his safe and took out a Colt Government .380: small, slim, light, and a perfect but smaller copy of the Colt 1911 .45. He also took out a shoulder holster and got it on, then he shoved the .380 into the holster and a spare magazine

11

next to it, then slipped into a tweed jacket. He tucked the envelope that Joan had prepared into an inside pocket.

It was a nice evening, so he didn't bother with his car and driver, finding a cab, instead. Ten minutes up Third Avenue, and he got out at Fifty-fifth Street and went into P. J. Clarke's.

The bar wasn't too crowded, since the five o'clockers had come and gone, and Dino wasn't there yet. He waved a finger at a bartender and the man produced a Knob Creek bourbon on the rocks. He took a sip, and before he could put the glass down, the bartender set another beside it, filled with a brown whiskey.

Dino picked it up. "Starting without me?"

"Only one sip ahead," he replied. "What have you learned about the list?"

"I'll tell you in the back room," Dino said, heading for the back room.

2

Stone handed Dino the envelope. "The originals are in there."

Dino pocketed it. "My evidence man thanks you."

"What have you learned about the list?"

"About as much as seventy cops and other employees can learn in the time since you called. There are a hundred and ten people who have these names and live or work or both in Manhattan, thirty-one are named John H. Williams, so it's not as bad as I thought it would be."

"What do they have in common?" Stone asked.

"You mean, besides being hunted by a lunatic?"

"He may have very good reasons," Stone said. "Did any of them know a lunatic who might want them dead?"

"There were a scattering of exes — wives and husbands, and just good friends — who

13

are candidates, but nobody who is known to any of the other survivors — so far. In fact, none of the names that anybody on the list came up with are known to any of the others."

"That would be too easy," Stone said.

"Of course, we haven't talked to you, yet." Dino handed him a sheet of paper with a lot of names typed on it. "These are all the people who are considered candidates for being the lunatic. Do you know any of them?"

Stone read through the list carefully. "Not a one," he said.

"No name says 'bingo!'?"

"None."

"All right, think about your circle of acquaintances: Do you know anyone who might want to kill you? And not just the women."

Stone got out his iPhone and scrolled through all the names on his contact list. "Nobody," he said.

"Well, I can think of one person," Dino said.

"And who might that be?"

"The first Mrs. Barrington," Dino said.

Stone sighed. Dino never missed an opportunity to bring up Dolce. She was the daughter of a close friend of Stone's, Eduardo Bianchi, now deceased, who had taken a keen interest in him, and he in her. They had been through a civil marriage ceremony in Venice, but before the scheduled church ceremony could be conducted, sealing the deal, Stone had been called back to the USA to help an old girlfriend who was considered a suspect in the death of her husband.

Dolce, incensed by his absence from Venice and the presence of a previous woman back in his life, had begun an obsessive campaign to get Stone back to the altar, and the whole thing had ended badly. Eduardo, understanding his daughter and fond of Stone, had retrieved the document that they had signed at the civil ceremony and returned it to Stone, who had, very quickly, set fire to it. Dolce now resided in a nunnery in Sicily, attended by the nuns, a number of guards, and at least one psychiatrist. "You know very well that Dolce is not free to attack me."

"I know that only because I spoke to my ex-wife this afternoon, who called the mother superior and ascertained that her sister is still 'in residence,' shall we say." Dino's ex-wife, Mary Ann, was Dolce's sister and, after their father's death, had been in charge of her treatment and confinement.

"Well, that's a relief," Stone said.

"You must admit that, if she had her freedom, she would be just the sort of person we're looking for."

"I suppose you're right. You'd like that, wouldn't you?"

"Sure I would. Just think of all the man-hours the department would save. As it is, we're having to interview every person whose name is on the list, and in addition, every ex-wife and ex-husband and ex-lover and all the crazy people whose names they gave us. Also, we've had to assign cops to protect them. God help us if we didn't protect every one of them and then that one turned up dead."

"Any luck with the adman?"

"No, both his secretary and his ex-wife, who know him better than anyone else, say he's just not of the nature to attract enemies. His name might as well have been drawn from a hat."

"Who are the others?"

"They're all employed in Manhattan by accounting or IT firms, universities, hospitals, etcetera, etcetera — no two of them with the same employer or even in the same field of endeavor. They're fairly high up in

16

their chosen fields, well-paid and well-thought of. About the only thing they have in common is that they're all single — either divorced or never married."

"Are any of the women lesbians or bisexual?"

"Only one, that we know of. She works on Page Six at the *Post,* dishing dirt. Why do you ask?"

"It occurred to me that the threat could have had affairs with all of them, if he or she were bisexual."

"Do you know any lesbians or bisexuals?" Dino asked.

"Not well enough for them to hate me," Stone replied.

"So your theory doesn't hold water?"

"I guess not."

They ordered steaks and wine.

"Oh," Dino said, "two of the people on the list, besides you, have carry licenses — one is a diamond merchant and one is a fancy pawnbroker, with offices in a Fifth Avenue skyscraper."

"Well, I'm packing, and I hope you told them to."

"We didn't have to; they both carry all the time."

Their steaks came, and they assaulted them.

17

"I get why the diamond merchant carries," Stone said, "but why the pawnbroker?"

"He says he has regular customers — for instance, a woman who's a handicapper at the track in her spare time, and when she loses, she gives him a call. She has a diamond ring worth two hundred grand, and she might borrow fifty on it. When she does, he takes the cash to her personally and collects the ring. The process reverses when she wins big."

"That's novel," Stone said.

"Yeah, he says he knows the ring better than he knows her."

"I guess we could hope that the perp picks one of those two pistol packers and gets his head blown off," Stone said.

"That would be nice," Dino said. "So to speak."

"Any other theories?"

"Yeah, there's one on the list who has, over some time, had multiple threats or attempts on his life."

"Which one?"

"Doesn't that sound familiar?"

"You're talking about *me*?"

"Why do you sound so shocked?"

"I've had . . . Well, there have been . . ."

"Yeah," Dino said. "I think about half of the guys in the Russian mafia carry a card with your photograph on it, just in case they spot you somewhere and get a shot at you."

"That's a gross exaggeration," Stone said.

"I know that's what you'd like to think, but it just ain't so."

"What's your point?" Stone asked.

"I think you'd better do more than pack a pistol, if you want to live through this little episode in your life."

"Are you offering me police protection?"

Dino shook his head. "Nah, you're too rich for that. You can hire your own."

3

Dino insisted on giving Stone a ride home in his armored SUV. "So," Dino said on the way, "let's talk about steps you need to take to stay alive."

"Oh, all right."

"The first step is for you to assume that you're the guy the lunatic is really after, and that all the others are camouflage."

"Okay, it can't hurt to assume that."

"Second thing is, you don't go out of the house unless it's absolutely necessary. And when you do, you get driven in your armored Bentley by Fred, who will also be packing." Fred was Stone's factotum and a dead shot.

"Fred always packs," Stone said.

"That's good," Dino said.

"What else should I do?"

"Well, if you get scared, leave the country; go to your house in England and keep your head down there. You're unique on the hit list in that you have an airplane capable of transatlantic flight and homes in two foreign countries."

"I can't argue with your reasoning," Stone said, as the car pulled up in front of the house, "but not yet."

Dino produced his weapon and rolled down his window. "All right, the coast appears to be clear; run for it, and I'll cover you."

Stone got out his own weapon, opened the car door, and ran for it. It took him longer than he would have liked to get out his key and open the door. He closed it behind him and took a couple of deep breaths before he went upstairs to bed.

He had just crawled into the sack when his phone rang. "Hello?"

"I hear you're in trouble again," a woman's voice said. It was Viv, Dino's wife, who was the COO of Strategic Services, the world's second-largest security company.

"Well, Dino thinks so, anyway. Where are you?"

"Hong Kong," she said. "I think. When I wake up in the morning I have to figure out where I am. Also, what day it is. Right now, because I've crossed the international date line, it's either tomorrow or yesterday, I can never remember which."

"I can understand your confusion."

"Dino says you need some protection, and I agree. I spoke to Mike Freeman — got hold of him just before he left on a round-the-globe tour of our international offices, and he'll have two people over there tomorrow morning."

"Have you seen the hit list?"

"Yeah, Dino e-mailed it to me."

"Any ideas about any of the names?"

"Well, if you're the target, it's got to be either a woman, her ex-husband, or her current boyfriend. It wouldn't be the first time."

"I'd like to argue with that, but I can't think of an argument."

"Well, apparently, you've accepted the fact that you're in jeopardy, and that's half the battle."

"I'd like to win the other half, too," Stone said.

"Then run scared; that's half of the other half of the battle. Remember the adman who thought he was just crossing the street when he took a round in the head."

"Yeah, he never knew what hit him or why," Stone said.

"I don't want that to happen to you, sweetie. If you got taken out we'd have to start paying for airplane flights and foreign vacations."

22

"Well, we don't want that to happen, do we?"

"Sleep tight, and watch your ass," Viv said, then hung up.

Stone reflected, as he hung up, that it was hard doing both those things at the same time.

The following morning, Stone was awakened a little earlier than he was accustomed to when the doorbell rang. He picked up his bedside phone and pushed the button. "Yes?"

"This is Frank Bender of Strategic Services," a gruff male voice said. "My partner and I are at your front door."

Why was the man telling him this? "Do you want to come inside?"

"Not at the moment. We'll stake out the two front doors for right now. After your people come to work, then we'll cover it from inside."

"Sounds good to me," Stone said. He hung up and put his head on the pillow. He was nearly asleep again when the doorbell fired again. "Yes?"

"It's Frank again. I forgot to ask: Are you armed?"

"To the teeth. Hold your questions for another hour, will you?"

"Sure."

Stone tried to go to sleep again, but he had been awake for too long, and his mind was at work. He called downstairs for breakfast and turned on the TV. An all-news-all-the-time channel was on, and his list was displayed on one side of the screen. "Here are the people the NYPD thinks may be in danger," the anchorwoman said. "If your name is on the list, and you live or work in Manhattan, you should have heard from the police by now. If you haven't, call them, for your own safety."

"Dino is just going to love this," Stone muttered to himself. His phone rang. "Hello?"

"Mr. Barrington, this is Henry Parker at Page Six; are you aware that your name is on a death list?"

"I watch TV, too," Stone replied. "Please don't call me again." He hung up. Immediately, the phone rang again.

"This is Henry Parker."

"Mr. Parker, do you remember calling me less than a minute ago?"

"Sure I do."

"Then you must remember what I said to you."

"You mean about not calling you again?"

"That's it, and yet you called me again."

24

"I just have a few questions," he said.

"Okay, I'm turning the phone off now." Stone hung up and flipped the switch that turned off all the phones on the fifth floor. Ten seconds later, his cell phone rang. Stone picked it up. "If you call me again, I'm going to come down there and shoot you," Stone said.

"Why would you want to shoot someone who has your life in his hands?" Dino asked.

"Oh, it's you. I thought it was that ass from Page Six."

"You might as well talk to him. Maybe people will stop calling when they know the *Post* has the story."

"Anything new?"

"Not a thing."

"Then why are you calling me in the middle of the night?" Stone asked.

"I just wanted to see if you were still alive, and it's six-thirty already," Dino said.

Stone hung up. His cell phone rang again. "Hello?"

"It's Dino. I have your cell phone number, you know."

"In that case," Stone said, "I'm turning it off." And he did so.

4

Stone was downstairs in his office by nine o'clock, and Joan was lying in wait for him. "Okay," she said. "Since I've watched the morning shows and read the papers and spoken to the two agents from Strategic Services, I think I fully grasp the situation."

"Good, I'm glad I don't have to explain it to you."

"Am I going to get to shoot somebody again?" Joan had once shot a man in Stone's office, who had been pointing a gun at him.

"If you're lucky," Stone said. "I know how much you enjoyed it last time."

"I'm locked and loaded," she replied, "even if I don't fully grasp what that means."

"You're not alone. Please try not to shoot anybody, unless he or she exhibits murderous intention."

"What would constitute an exhibition of 'murderous intention'?" she asked.

"Pointing a weapon at you — or worse, at me."

"Got it."

"Oh, remember all the paperwork and questioning you had to deal with last time?"

"I do."

"That's a good reason for not firing unless you're really convinced of murderous intention."

"I'll try not to be too trigger-happy," she said, then went back to her office. She came back almost immediately. "There's another guy here from Strategic Services, says he wants to check all the security equipment to make sure it's working."

"Check his ID, then set him loose in the house."

She left. A moment later a man in coveralls, carrying a toolbox, came into his office and unceremoniously began checking the phone and electrical boxes, working from a plan of the house. When he was done, he left the office without a word and began to work his way around the house.

Stone's iPhone rang and he picked it up.

"Scramble," Lance Cabot said. The man was the director of Central Intelligence, and Stone had recently been appointed a personal advisor to him, holding the rank of deputy director.

27

"Scrambled," Stone replied.

"What kind of mess have you got yourself into now?" Lance asked pleasantly.

"I'm not sure what kind of mess it is," Stone replied, "except I'm advised by the NYPD that it could be fatal. I know only that I have no idea what's going on."

"You're a constant source of amusement to me, Stone."

"I'm so happy to hear that, Lance. I'm glad to provide you with amusement."

"Are the press reports accurate?"

"For once, and regrettably, yes. I think Dino must have thought it in the interests of keeping the people on that list, including me, alive."

"Are you sure about that?"

"No, but he and I and Joan are the only people of my acquaintance who were aware of the list. Except you, of course; you seem to be aware of everything."

"And now that knowledge has been expanded to the world at large."

"Exactly."

"You shouldn't leave the house, you know."

"Lance, I've already had that conversation with Dino, and I think he covered all the bases. And there are two armed people from Strategic Services in the house, and one of their technicians, as well, to check all the security equipment."

"You should locate that technician immediately," Lance said, "and shoot him."

"Why would I do anything so inhospitable to a person who is trying to protect me?"

"Stone, if you can remember as far back as a few weeks ago, you may recall that Agency people replaced all your security equipment with our own."

"I guess Strategic Services didn't get the memo," Stone replied.

"And before that, all your equipment was installed and managed by your friend Bob Cantor. It has been some years since Stratigic Services has had anything to do with it."

Stone thought for moment. "Oh, shit," he said.

"I called to tell you that my people will be there within the hour to perform that service. Now, go find that tech guy and shoot him." Lance hung up.

"Joan!" Stone yelled.

Joan stuck her head inside the door. "Yes, sir?"

"Tell the Strategic Service people that there's an intruder in the house, disguised as one of their technical service guys, and

29

they should apprehend or shoot him right now!"

"Holy shit!" Joan yelled, as she ran back to her office.

Stone, who had not bothered to carry a weapon, since he had had no intention of leaving the house, now opened his office safe, retrieved a Sig Arms 9mm pistol, racked the slide, grabbed a spare magazine, and sat down at his desk again, the pistol in his hand.

Joan entered, waving her .45 around. "They're on it, boss!" she said.

"I asked you to check his ID," Stone reminded her.

"I did. It looked good to me."

"Lance is sending some CIA people over to check everything out. Don't shoot them, and compare their faces to the photos on their IDs."

"Right!"

"And keep them in your office until Frank and his partner check back with us. We don't want them shooting the Agency people and vice versa."

"Right."

The outside doorbell rang. Joan ran back in that direction and then came back a couple of minutes later. "It's the Agency people," she said. "I checked them out, then called Lance to confirm."

"Just sit them down, for the moment."

Five minutes later, there was a shout from the other side of the door to the garage. "Mr. Barrington?"

"Who are you?" Stone shouted back.

"It's Frank. May I come in?"

"Holster your weapon before you do," Stone yelled.

The door opened, and Frank stuck his empty hands inside.

"All right," Stone said, "come in."

Frank entered the room, followed by a woman in a business suit. "This is my partner, Grace," Frank said. "We've cleared every room. The kitchen door to the garden was ajar. Is there a way to the street from the garden?"

"Yes, across the garden, on the Second Avenue side there's a gate."

"Then he must have left that way. You're going to need to have the people who installed your equipment come back and take a look at it."

"They're waiting in Joan's office," Stone replied. "Don't shoot them."

5

The CIA technician came into Stone's office and took the chair across the desk from him. "Well, that guy — whoever he was — knew what he was doing. He did a great job of fucking up your security system."

"Did you do a great job of fixing it?" Stone asked.

"We did. We've tested it in every operating mode, and everything now works."

"Would you say that whoever the guy was, he's familiar with CIA equipment and installations?"

The man stared back at Stone for half a minute. "Could be," he said, finally. "But any genius could have done what he did."

"So I'm dealing with a genius?"

"At the very least, you're dealing with somebody who knows how to hire a genius."

"That's not encouraging," Stone said.

"No, it's not."

"Anything else I can do for you?" Stone asked.

"See if your secure cell phone works."

Stone got the thing out and pressed the appropriate buttons. "Scramble," he said into the phone. He got an immediate confirmation from Lance Cabot. "It works," Stone said to the CIA tech.

"Then I bid you a cheery good day," the man replied, and he and his partner departed.

"Did my people fix it?" Lance asked.

"Yes, and they were very impressed with the guy who screwed it up, implying that he was familiar with CIA equipment and installations."

"That's libelous," Lance replied.

"No, it's just innocent conjecture, based on the available evidence."

"So, it's working now?"

"Can you hear me?"

"Loud and clear."

"It's working." Stone hurried to hang up first.

Joan came into his office, still carrying her .45. "Is it fixed?"

"It's fixed. You can put that cannon away now."

"Not on your life," she said. "They'll be back."

"What makes you think that?"

"Well, the guy was interrupted and came close to getting shot. I shouldn't think he'd be happy with how he left things."

"The CIA guy thought he should be very pleased with himself," Stone said.

"He's just annoyed that an outsider could screw up his equipment."

"Maybe the outsider is a former insider. He was only here — How long?"

"I don't know; twenty minutes, maybe a little longer."

"Then he knew exactly where to go, didn't he? He had some plans rolled up, tucked under his arm. Describe him for me."

"I don't know," Joan said, wrinkling her brow, "medium size, uh . . ."

"I can't describe him, either," Stone said. "He didn't call attention to himself, never said a word."

"I hope he's smarter than his boss," Joan said.

"He may *be* the boss," Stone replied, "but I didn't know him. Dino thinks I know the culprit."

"He sure didn't ring a bell with me, either."

"Call Mike Freeman and tell him I want two more people over here — one at the kitchen door at all times. The guy knows about that door, and the gate to the street."

"Mike left this morning to fly around the world. He'll be gone a week or three."

"Then find the next guy in line — no the next guy in line is Viv, and she's in Hong Kong. Find the guy after her."

"Where do you want the other guy?"

"Moving around the house. Make sure he knows who lives and works here. You've got photographs, right?"

"A regular album."

"Good." His phone rang, and he picked it up. "Hello?"

"It's Dino. How's your day going?"

"Not so hot," Stone replied, then brought him up to date.

"I guess you're going to blame me for releasing the list to the press."

"It crossed my mind, but I don't think the perp learned anything he didn't already know."

"You want me to send cops?"

"Tell you what, send me a cop car and park it at the curb. That should accomplish the job while not straining your budget."

"I can do that," Dino said.

"When will it be here?"

"As soon as you can look out the window and see it."

"Listen, have it delivered by two uniforms,

and tell them to enter the house through the business entrance. They can go out the kitchen door and across the gardens to the Second Avenue exit. That way, if we're being surveilled, the perp will think the cops are stationed inside."

"Don't slow them down," Dino said. "I need the manpower."

"We'll hide the donuts. Since I can't go out, you want to come over here for dinner tonight?"

"Sure, why not."

"Be sure to tell your driver to park out front."

"Yeah, yeah." Dino hung up.

6

Stone got a call on his cell phone; caller ID read: VANESSA BAKER. He hesitated to answer, then did anyway.

"Hi, there," he said. "How are you? Vanessa had recently been an inadvertent target of a poisoner but seemed fully recovered now.

"You didn't come to the funeral," she said. The funeral she referred to had been that of her mother, who had been involved with a Russian spy group that had been raided by CIA personnel. Betty Baker had been shot and died on the spot.

"I'm afraid that was deliberate," Stone said.

"A lot of other people didn't show up, either — people she thought of as her friends. There was no public announcement, but I sent out an e-mail notice of the time and place."

"I got it, and I apologize for not respond-
ing."

"Hardly anyone else did, either."

"Vanessa, has it occurred to you that she
wasn't anybody's friend? She committed
treason, and even if she had lived through
the raid she would have been convicted and
sentenced to death. At least, she was spared
that fate."

"I suppose you're right," she said.
"Frankly, I wouldn't have been there myself,
except that she was my mother, and I loved
her."

"I can understand that. Dino and I are
having dinner here tonight. Would you like
to join us?"

She didn't hesitate. "I'd love to. I need to
get out of the house."

"It's casual, come at six-thirty for drinks."

"All right. See you then." She hung up.

He buzzed Joan and asked her to let Helene, his housekeeper and cook, know they'd
be three for dinner.

His cell phone rang again, and he picked
it up. "Scramble," Lance said.

Stone scrambled. "Yes?"

"I had a word with our tech guy who
straightened out your security system. He
tends to agree with you, that your interloper
might, indeed, have worked for us at one

38

time. He says that you said the man had plans of the house."

"That is so," Stone replied. "Where else could he have gotten those, except from the people who did the work, namely you and yours?"

"I've got people working on the records of everybody who has left us in the past few years."

"It occurs to me that he could have been a member of the team who installed the equipment," Stone said.

"That occurred to us as well, and the thought makes me very uncomfortable."

"You must have people leave you all the time for work in the private sector," Stone said.

"Yes, but not as many as you might think. Our people who are contentedly employed here tend to stay for the pension. They're civil servants, after all. It's those who are malcontented in some way — maybe they've been treated in ways they think are harsh; maybe they didn't get a promotion they wanted, that sort of thing."

"Understandable," Stone said. "Let me know what you come up with."

"I'm sure you'll be speaking to Dino," Lance said. "Please ask him to send me the

ballistics report in the case of the dead adman."

"All right."

Lance hung up.

That evening, Dino arrived first. Stone
passed on Lance's request for the ballistics
report.

"I think you and Lance could be on the
right track," Dino said. "A witness to the
shooting said the pistol was silenced, and
I'm sure Lance's armory is bulging with
that sort of thing. I'll get the report to him
first thing in the morning."

The doorbell rang, and Stone checked the
video screen on the phone before buzzing
in Vanessa. He greeted her at the study
door, then fixed her a drink. She and Dino
embraced.

"I'm sorry about your mother," he said.

"Thank you."

"Did you have a lot of press at the funeral?"

"No, the incident doesn't seem to have
made the papers yet. I guess Lance is keeping it quiet, and I'm grateful for that."

"How are you feeling?" Dino asked.

"Perfectly normal, physically," she said,
"but a little depressed."

"That's to be expected in the circumstances," he said.

Stone fixed Dino another drink, and Fred appeared in the doorway. "Dinner at seven," he said.

"Thank you, Fred."

"I read in the paper about this list Stone got," Vanessa said. "Have you two made any headway on that?"

"Not yet," Stone said. He told her about the security tech.

"That's scary," she said.

"Lance is working on it from his end. He thinks the man might be ex-Agency."

"No," Dino said, "that's what *you* think."

"Let's just say that Lance is coming around to my way of thinking," Stone replied.

Dinner arrived, one of Helene's Greek creations that everyone enjoyed.

"Stone," Vanessa said, "do you think the Russians could be behind this death-list thing?"

Stone shook his head. "I don't think so. After all, the only Russian I've had anything to do with lately is Yevgeny Chekhov, and Lance has him locked up."

"Locked up where?" Dino asked.

"My best guess is Guantánamo," Stone said.

"Then he's been out of touch with his fellow countrymen since Lance's people arrested him on his yacht."

"I expect so," Stone said. "Though it was more like a kidnapping. Lance must have had a plane waiting."

They were on coffee in the study when Dino's phone went off, and he answered it. "Bacchetti. Where? Be there in five." He hung up. "You're going to have to excuse me, but we've got another hit from your list."

"I want to come," Vanessa said.

"So do I," Stone echoed, rising.

"No," Dino said. "It will shock you, Vanessa, and it will bore Stone. I won't be long. This is currently our most visible case, and I have to make an appearance. Save me some dessert."

Dino left, and they sat down again, Vanessa in Stone's lap. "I'm glad Dino's gone," she said. "I've missed you."

Stone kissed her, then picked her up and set her next to him on the sofa. "Dino's coming back. We don't want to start something now and shock him when he walks in."

7

Vanessa ignored his instructions and climbed back aboard, straddling him. "I'm not wearing any underwear," she said, going for his belt buckle. Before he could stop her he was inside her.

"There!" she said, moving slowly.

"You're too quick for me," he said, helping.

"I am. Remember that."

"How could I forget it?"

They were at the point of climax when the doorbell rang.

"Don't answer it yet," she said, moving faster.

"Dino has a key," Stone replied. "Ringing the bell was his way of being polite." He picked her up and set her aside again, adjusted his clothing, and managed to be pouring three brandies when Dino walked in, having made coughing noises as he crossed toward the study.

43

"Gee, I hope one of those is for me," he said.

Stone handed them each a snifter and took one for himself. He buzzed Helene and told her that now was a good time for dessert.

Dino reached over and adjusted Stone's necktie. "There, that's better," he said. "I hope."

"Everything is fine, Dino," Stone replied. "Now, tell us what happened."

"Trisha Marshall happened," Dino. "Number nine on your list, right before you."

"Where?"

"Would you believe the ice rink at Rockefeller Center, and with two cops watching her?"

"You have cops on skates?"

"Not exactly," Dino replied. "They were watching from the perimeter when she seemed to trip and fall. Then they saw the blood. They both fell down, running across the ice. She'd taken a round in the back of the neck at the top of the spine. She never knew what hit her."

"Anybody hear a shot?"

"No, but it came from above, at street level, and nobody heard anything or saw it fired. At this time of night the crowds are thinning out."

"Please add the ballistics report on that one to the other one you're sending to Lance."

"Sure. It's gotta be from the same gun."

"And the gun is probably from Lance's armory, down in technical services at Langley."

"Let's not get too far ahead of ourselves," Dino said.

Fred entered with a tray of Greek pastries, rich with honey, and gave them forks.

"It's a good hypothesis, and you know it," Stone said.

"We're not going to make an immediate announcement," Dino said.

"You won't have to. Type is being set as we speak, and I'll bet there were three TV trucks there before you left."

"Four," Dino said, "but all NBC had to do was walk across the street."

Stone reached for the TV remote control, but Dino held up a hand. "Don't please; I've already seen it, and you can wait until tomorrow morning."

"Have you thought about a copycat?" Stone said. "After all, a series of murders is an invitation to anybody who'd like to knock off a spouse or an ex."

"It crossed my mind, but it's too soon.

45

Maybe after the next one."

Vanessa spoke up. "You think there'll be a next one?"

"As sure as brandy follows coffee," Stone said, pouring them more.

"There's always an opportunist out there," Dino said.

"Or two," Stone added.

"God forbid." Dino's phone went off again. He checked the caller ID, then switched off the instrument. "I don't know how these people get my cell number, but they do, inevitably."

"Next thing you know," Stone said, "they'll be ringing the doorbell."

"Nobody knows where I am but my driver."

The doorbell rang.

Stone picked up the phone. "Yes?"

"Commissioner Bacchetti, please."

"Wrong house, wrong time of day," Stone said, then hung up.

"That was my driver," Dino said, getting to his feet. "I turned off my cell, so he had to ring the bell." He tossed off the remainder of his brandy. "I'm going to go home and hide there," he said. "Tell Helene it was a wonderful dinner, as always, and you two sleep well. Or something." He departed.

Vanessa climbed aboard again. "Where

were we?"

"Why don't we work on that in an actual bed," Stone replied. He picked her up and headed for the elevator.

The following morning, when Stone turned on the TV, the media were all over the killing. NBC had a shot from the top of 30 Rock that zoomed in from thirty stories up, framing the corpse surrounded by white coats and blue uniforms, then zooming slowly in. Finally, they showed the remains being loaded on a gurney and then crossing the street to an underground elevator, the press figured it out in time to be hot on the heels of the wagon as it drove away.

They cut to an anchorwoman: "The police have made no statement yet, but our sources tell us that the victim was number nine on the hit list that's been in the news. If so, her name is Trisha Marshall, and she's a researcher at the *New Yorker* magazine. She's forty-nine, divorced with two college-age children, and a regular at the Rockefeller Center skating rink."

Stone switched channels and got more of the same. "My kingdom for some political reportage," Stone said aloud.

Vanessa stirred. "What?"

"Nothing on TV except last night's killing

47

at 30 Rock," Stone said.

"What time is it?"

"Breakfast time. What's your pleasure?"

"French toast, bacon, OJ, and coffee," she muttered, then turned over and went back to sleep.

Stone phoned the order to Helene in the kitchen, then retrieved the *Times* from outside his bedroom door, where it appeared, magically, each morning. The *Times* had placed the story, discretely, at the bottom of page one, where lived the one-sentence headlines of the stories continued inside. Stone went straight for the crossword.

Breakfast arrived in the dumbwaiter; Stone set the tray on the bed and poked at Vanessa's ass with a finger.

"Huh?"

"French toast," Stone replied. "Better eat it now, while it's hot. And you can pass up that punch line."

8

Stone had packed Vanessa off home and was at his desk, when Lance phoned and scrambled.

"Good morning," Stone said.

"And to you. Dino got the two ballistics reports to us overnight, and both victims were killed with the same weapon."

"That's to be expected," Stone said. "Question is: What is the origin of the weapon?"

"I know what you're thinking, and I considered it myself for a while, but it is not from our armory, nor is it a personal weapon registered with us by an employee, which is a firm requirement."

"Any other thoughts?" Stone asked.

"Somebody else's armory," Lance said.

"What about somebody's workshop?" Stone queried.

"That's a possibility, if he had good tools. He wouldn't have to make the guns; he could buy those. But the silencers? That would make sense."

"So, anybody with a basement, a standing drill, threading tools, and a selection of hard bits could have made the silencers?"

"A wide net, isn't it."

"Something to look for if he's captured by other means," Stone said.

"Search warrants are Dino's métier, not mine. So, for that matter, is murder. Why am I involved? I forget."

"Because one of your ex-people came to my house with a tool kit and did some damage."

"Ex-people. I like that, like ex-wives and ex-dogs. A divorced colleague of mine used to refer to his kids as his ex-children."

"He sounds heartless enough to be one of yours," Stone commented.

"The most softhearted man you could imagine," Lance replied.

"Who, in your shop, could have had access to the plans of my house?" Stone asked.

"Interesting question. The answer is: anybody with a computer and a password, or the ability to figure one out. Did you know that the most popular password among computer users is 1-2-3-4-5-6-7-8? The second most popular is *password*. Or maybe it's the other way around."

"I'm not going to tell you what mine is," Stone said.

"You'd be easy. Something to do with your airplane, I'll bet."

"Stop guessing," Stone said, making a mental note to himself to change all of his passwords.

"You know," Lance said, "you should come out of retirement as a homicide detective and work full time on this problem. After all, you're on the hit list yourself."

"I seem to be doing that without even trying," Stone said. His desk phone buzzed; he picked it up and Joan said, "Dino on one."

"Gotta run," Stone said to Lance. Then he hung up his cell phone and pressed line one on his desk phone. "I'm here," he said.

"Have you talked to Lance yet this morning?"

"Yes, just. He told me both people were killed with the same weapon, and it wasn't one of the Agency's."

"You want to come down here and work on this? I'll find you a desk."

"Thanks, but no thanks. I've had enough bad coffee and stale donuts to last me a lifetime. I'll lend you my brain, such as it is, from time to time."

"Great, I'll send somebody over to remove it. See ya." Dino hung up.

51

Stone pressed another button on the desk phone.

"Yes, sir?" Joan said.

"Change all our computer passwords," he said.

"Change them to what?"

"My father's middle name, plus two exclamation points."

"And what would that be?"

"Check my birth certificate. If you enter it incorrectly, we'll have to buy all new computers."

"Certainly."

His cell phone rang. Vanessa. "Good morning again."

"I enjoyed the first one more," she said.

"Any time."

"I really needed you last night. You lifted the gloom."

"What are you doing today?"

"I'm down at the shop, cleaning out my mother's office."

"I don't think you should do that. Have you already started?"

"Only a moment ago. Why shouldn't I?"

"Because of what Betty had been doing for many years. Lance is going to want to see every scrap of paper and, especially, the contents of the safe. I'll get him to send some people over."

"Well, I don't know the combination to her safe, so tell him to send me a safe-cracker, too."

"I'll do that."

"What are you doing for lunch?" she asked, and there was a leer in her voice.

"Oh, no you don't."

"Why not?"

"You're overestimating my physical properties."

"I've inspected your physical properties carefully, and I find them sufficient to my needs."

"But they are insufficient to your desires," he declared. "Wait until this evening, anyway."

"Six-thirty?"

"Fine. I'll try to get in a restorative nap before then." They hung up.

Stone called Lance and scrambled.

"Yes?"

"Vanessa was about to clean out her mother's office, but I stopped her, thinking your people might like to examine the contents thereof."

"Funny you should think of that," Lance said, "there's a team on its way to her offices as we speak."

"Oh, and she doesn't know the combination to her mother's safe; says you should send a yegg."

"Most people write down the combination and tape it to the bottom of a desk drawer, or some similar place. They'll look for it there, before we send a safecracker."

"As you wish. Goodbye." He hung up, knowing that Lance was looking for somebody to send.

A couple of hours passed, and Lance called back.

"Well, we went over Betty's office," he said.

"Find anything?"

"The combination of the safe, taped to the bottom of a file drawer."

"And what were its contents?"

"Stacks of dollars and euros, mostly."

"She was ready to get out, then?"

"At all times," Lance said, "save when we actually came calling on the Vineyard."

"Did you find anything else of value?"

"No, but my team is on the way to her apartment now, and that could be more productive."

"Good luck to you, then." He hung up.

9

He picked up Vanessa at her apartment and was given a drink.

"You were right," she said. "Those CIA — at least, I think that's who they were — people turned up at my offices a couple of hours after you called."

"What did they find?"

"A whole lot of money in the safe. I heard one of them say there was more than two hundred thousand dollars, some of it in euros. And do you know what?"

"What?"

"They took it away."

"Did they give you a receipt?"

"Yes, but only because I demanded one, or I said I would call the police and charge them with burglary."

Stone laughed. "I like that," he said. "Would you like me to see if I can get it back from them?"

"Would I ever! I was thinking of a grand

European vacation."

"Where in Europe?"

"Wherever my little heart desires."

"Well, you're not going to get the actual banknotes back, but would you take a check?"

"As long as it doesn't bounce."

"Let me have your receipt."

She dug into her purse and came up with a piece of notepaper that had been ripped from a pocket ring binder.

"Ray Rodriguez," he read, peering at the receipt. "Or is it Roy?" They couldn't tell. "I'll call Lance tomorrow. Oh, do you have any actual cash in your purse?"

"What do you need?" she asked, rummaging.

"Whataya got? A buck will do."

"The smallest I've got is a ten."

"That'll be ten dollars, please."

She handed it to him but didn't release her end. "Ten dollars for what?"

"Legal representation."

"Do I need a lawyer?"

"Do you want your mother's ill-gotten gains back?"

"Sure."

"Then you need a lawyer."

"Okay, but you'd better be worth it."

"I'm keeping it whether I am or not.

That's how lawyers make a living."

"I think you should institute a money-back guarantee."

"Then I'd starve to death."

"You know, I'm starving to death right now. Where are we going?"

"To Caravaggio."

"I love that place."

Gianni, the old headwaiter from Elaine's, greeted them and sat them down, then brought drinks and menus.

"That is one magnificent nose over there," Vanessa said.

Stone didn't look up. "At the first table? Heroic, I'd call it."

"How'd you know?"

"He's said to be an ancient Mafioso, and I think every time I've been in here he's had that table," Stone replied.

"Maybe he owns the place."

"Could be," Stone said. "He certainly owns that table, at the very least."

"Oh, Dino just came in," she said. "Are we expecting him?"

"No, but be nice to him. Dino stopped and shook the hand of the ancient Mafioso, then continued to their table, where he unceremoniously sat down and received a large scotch from Gianni. "We got a tiny break," he said.

"I'll take whatever you've got," Stone said.

"This afternoon a woman who works as a secretary at NBC took her lunch outside and was leaning against the parapet that surrounds the ice rink when she saw something at her feet. It turned out to be an empty .45 shell casing, and she recovered it."

"Did she mess it up?"

"No, she watches a lot of TV, so she picked it up with a pencil and took it to the nearest cop, who placed it in an evidence bag and called his precinct."

"Any prints?"

"A piece of an index finger," Dino said. "It may be enough for a search. They're running it now."

"What brings you uptown, Dino?" he asked.

"I thought you'd like to know about the shell casing. It's all part of the service."

"I'm impressed," Stone said.

"You should be."

"Also, I'm not impressed."

"Why not?"

"Why didn't your people find the shell casing after the shooting? Apparently it was lying there, in plain sight."

Dino looked uncomfortable, even

58

squirmed a bit.

"I mentioned that to the captain in charge of the investigation," he said. "He turned red."

"Well, at least he has some shame."

"And we have the shell casing!" Dino crowed. His cell phone rang, and he answered it. "Bacchetti." He listened for a moment. "How many times was she shot? Oh. Thanks, keep up the good work." He hung up.

"I take it there were no prints," Stone said.

"Like I said, there was half a print."

"Did they run it?"

"Yeah, but nothing popped up. The tech says he thinks it's a woman's print."

"How do you tell a woman's print from a man's?"

"Smaller, I guess. Anyway, if we make an arrest, we'll have some fingers to compare it to."

"There's always that," Stone said.

"I think the print belongs to one of yours," Dino said after a moment.

"One of my what?"

"Women. The fact that it's a woman points to you."

"First of all," Stone said, "you don't know it's a woman's print. Tell me that after you're in possession of an actual finger that's a match, one that's attached to a woman."

"You don't believe in hunches, do you?" Dino asked.

"Only when they're revealed to be true by means of actual facts."

"Picky, picky, picky."

"And even if they are, you're going to be wrong at least half the time."

Dino polished off his drink and stood up. "I don't know why I bothered to come here and tell you this," he said.

"Because you wanted to brag about something," Stone replied.

"Vanessa, good evening, and my sympathies for having to put up with company like this." He turned and walked out of the restaurant.

"You were very rude to Dino," Vanessa said.

"That wasn't rude; I was just keeping him in line. He was acting as if he'd cracked the case. Half a print!"

10

The following morning, Stone and Vanessa conducted one more inspection of each other's physical properties, declared themselves satisfied, and put the equipment to work.

An hour later, shaved, showered, dressed, and just a little tired, Stone sat down at his desk and called Lance.

"Scramble," he said.

"Scrambled. What is it, Stone?"

"A lady of my acquaintance wishes to cash a check."

"Send her to a bank."

"You are her bank."

"What?"

"She has, let's see" — he dug out the receipt — "two hundred and twelve thousand dollars, some of it in euros, on deposit with your firm. She'd like to cash a check in that amount and have it sent to her now."

"The cash of which you speak is evidence," Lance said.

"Come now, you're not the police department; you said so yourself just the other day. You have no legal basis for confiscating her funds, and she wants them back."

"They're not her funds, they're her mother's."

"You say that as though you think you have a right to her mother's cash. It's my client's, by virtue of a probate-proof will and trust."

"Her mother was an espionage agent for a foreign, unfriendly government."

"Did you bring any charges against her?"

"We were about to when she started shooting at us."

"Then she has never been charged with a crime, and you can't demonstrate that the source of her funds is an illegal one."

"We're still processing that money," Lance said. "It's going to take some time, quite a lot of it."

"Process it all you like," Stone said. "My client will take your check."

"You want me to issue her a CIA check for $212,000?"

"She's not asking for a loan, Lance. It's her money, remember?"

"This is highly irregular."

"What's irregular is your people barging

62

into her office without a search warrant, breaking into her safe, and taking her money. *That's* highly irregular. Refunding it is highly regular."

"Hold on a minute; I need to speak to one of our drudges in accounting."

Stone put his feet up on his desk and sighed deeply. Sooner than he had expected, Lance returned to the call.

"All right, the check will be on my desk in ten minutes, made out to . . . ?"

"To the Woodman & Weld trust account and to me."

"When would you like to pick it up?" Lance asked.

"Allow me to introduce the Central Intelligence Agency to Federal Express," Stone said. "They have a nifty little overnight delivery service."

"And you're paying for it?"

"No, the institution who appropriated the funds is paying the cost of restoring them to their rightful owner."

"Oh, all right. Here's the check now. I'm signing it."

"Just send it to my office."

"Lunch is on you next time, and I'm choosing the wine." Lance hung up.

Stone buzzed Joan. "There's a check for $212,000 coming from Lance tomorrow morning. Please deposit it in the trust account and issue a check on our account in the same amount to Vanessa Baker. Give her check to me right away."

"Yes, sir, boss. Doing a little money laundering, are we?"

"It's all legal and aboveboard," Stone said. "Well, legal, anyway. Nothing those people do is aboveboard."

Joan came in a couple of minutes later with the freshly minted check, waving it in the breeze, as if to dry the ink.

Stone accepted the check, looked at the amount, signed it, and placed it in an envelope.

"You think we could do a couple hundred grand for me like that?" Joan asked.

"Of course. All you have to do is to persuade Lance Cabot to send me another check in any amount that appeals to you, then you can write yourself a check, and I'll sign it."

"I was hoping we could eliminate the red tape," she said, then went back to her office.

Vanessa came into his office a little later. "I'm going to do some shopping, and it's starting to rain outside. May I borrow Fred and the Bentley for a couple of hours?"

"Of course. I'm having lunch in." He

handed her the envelope. "This might help with your shopping."

She looked at it suspiciously, then opened it. "Holy shit!" she said.

"That was very unladylike," Stone admonished.

"You mean I can just hand this to Bergdorf's?"

"I think it might be less alarming and more convenient for both you and Bergdorf's if you use your credit card, deposit the check, and pay the bill when it comes."

"I can do that."

"And before you start buying sable coats and diamond necklaces, remember that you're planning a European tour with some of that money."

"Oh, yeah. Can I borrow your airplane for that?"

"Yes, but I'll have to come along and see that you don't scratch the paint."

"You will be welcome," she said.

Joan stuck her head through the door. "Fred is waiting in the garage for Vanessa."

"You are psychic," Stone said.

"I phoned her before I came down," Vanessa interjected. She gave him a big, wet kiss and ran for the garage.

"Joan, will you get me Mike Freeman, please?"

"Sure thing, boss." She went back to her office. A minute later she buzzed. "Mike Freeman on one."

Stone pressed the button. "Good morning," he said.

"Good evening," Mike replied.

"Where are you?"

"Just left Dubai, now over the Indian Ocean, bound for Singapore."

"Ah, I forgot you're doing your annual office tour."

"Not annual, exactly; just when I get bored. Want to join us in Singapore and fly home with us?"

"It's too far to the airport," Stone replied. "Have you heard about the hit list?"

"Of course, I have. I'm not *that* far away."

"The other day we had a technician in the house to go over my security system," Stone said. "Did you hear about that?"

"No, and what's more, we don't do your security system anymore."

"That's why Lance Cabot told me to shoot the man when he heard about him. He was sporting a Strategic Services ID, probably fake."

"It's impossible to fake our ID," Mike said.

"I thought maybe he might have once worked for you."

"Name?"

"I'm afraid we failed to make note of that."

"Description?"

"Too ordinary to remember."

"You're very unhelpful."

"Next time you call the office, could you ask if you have an ex-employee with the animus and skills to screw up my security system?"

"Sure. I'll be calling in tomorrow."

"I'd appreciate that."

"Oh, someone has just handed me your hit list."

"Does it interest you?"

"It certainly does. All the people whose names —"

The phone sputtered and went dead. Stone buzzed Joan. "Yes, sir?"

"I was cut off speaking to Mike Freeman. Can you get him back for me?"

"Of course."

Stone tapped his fingers on his desk while he was waiting.

"Boss?"

"I'm here. Mike?"

"He's not on. I tried several times and then got a message saying — hang on, I've got it right here. 'This satellite telephone cannot be accessed at this time, due to satellite realignment. Please try again in a few hours.' Shall I try again later?"

"Never mind," Stone said. "Get me Viv Bacchetti, instead."

"Sure thing." Minutes passed. "Boss?"

"Viv?"

"No, sir. She's en route from Hong Kong to Singapore, and I got the same message when I tried her satphone."

"Oh, the hell with it," he said, then hung up.

Dino called. "Dinner?"

"Sure, can I bring Vanessa?"

"I'd much prefer it if you did. I'd rather look at her than you. Seven at Patroon." He hung up.

11

Stone and Vanessa arrived at Patroon to find Dino waiting for them. She gave him a big kiss on the forehead.

"Hey, baby," he said. "Hey to you, too," he said to Stone, "but no kissing."

"Not even on the forehead?" Stone asked.

"Shut up and drink." Dino had already ordered for them, and their drinks arrived and were attacked.

"You make any progress on the 30 Rock shooting?" Stone asked.

"Oh, I love hearing sentences like that," Vanessa said. "It's like reading Raymond Chandler or Elmore Leonard."

"Stone can't talk that good," Dino said.

"And to answer my question . . . ?"

"Your answer is: not much."

"Does that mean a little or nothing at all?"

"Take your pick."

"Oh, you're such tough guys!" Vanessa laughed.

69

Dino patted her hand. "We've had thousands of hours of rehearsal in patrol cars," he said.

"Seems more like millions," Stone said. "I tried to call your wife today, and . . ."

"And you got a recorded message about satellite realignment," Dino said. "Personally, I think the North Koreans have shot down a couple of those birds over Asia. Why did you want to talk to my wife? Are you two having an affair?"

"She's in Singapore by this time. How could we be having an affair?"

"Phone sex," Dino said.

"Better than no sex at all," Vanessa chimed in.

"I was talking to Mike when the sat system went down, so I tried her, instead. He was about to say something meaningful about the hit list when we were cut off."

"What was he saying?"

"How would I know? We were cut off."

"What did he say before you were cut off?"

"He said he'd heard about the list, and then he started to say something about it, and then, *pfffft!*"

"Well," Dino said, looking at his watch. "It's tomorrow morning — or this morning — over there. I can never remember which."

"That's what Viv said."

"You said you couldn't reach her," Dino replied.

"I spoke to her before she left Hong Kong," Stone said. "Phone sex."

"You were talking dirty to my wife?"

"I don't consider sex to be dirty, just because it's over the phone."

"Hear, hear," Vanessa said.

"Vanessa sounds like she's in the House of Lords," Dino said.

Stefan, the headwaiter, arrived with menus. "I hope I'm interrupting something important," he said. "What would you like tonight?"

"Well, first of all," Stone said, "we want to watch you make a Caesar salad, then I'd like the Dover sole."

"Me, too!" Dino and Vanessa said simultaneously.

"And a bottle of the Puligny-Montrachet," Stone said. Stefan vanished and then returned with a cart bearing a wooden salad bowl, romaine lettuce, egg yolks, olive oil, lemon juice, raw garlic, Parmigiano Reggiano, and anchovies. He donned a skullcap. "Required by law," he explained. Shortly, he had done his magic with the ingredients and they were munching contentedly, if noisily.

They were finished with their sole and contemplating dessert when Stone's cell phone rang.

"I'll bet it's Lance," Dino said. "Better answer it, and ask him if the North Koreans have shot down some satellites."

Stone answered, and they scrambled.

"How was your Dover sole?" Lance asked.

"Stop that, Lance. It's like you have a tiny satellite circling my head and reporting back to you."

"How odd you should mention that."

Dino leaned in. "Lance, have the North Koreans shot down any satellites today over China?"

Lance was stonily silent for a long moment. Then, "How did you know that, Dino? It's highly classified."

"What?"

"I'm going to have to send some people over there to arrest you," Lance said, "before you leak that information to somebody who shouldn't know it."

"Like the North Koreans?"

"Exactly," Lance said. "You'll be picked up before you finish dessert. Now, Stone, can we put aside this nonsense, or have

Dino restrained, so that we can talk serious business?"

"Good idea about Dino," Stone said. "Shoot. Oh, Vanessa's here, too. Can you trust her?"

"Send her to the ladies'," Lance said.

"You hear that?" Stone asked her.

She hipped her way out of the booth. "Oh, all right. I'm not wanted, I'll go."

"She's gone," Stone said. "What's up?"

"Just a moment," Lance said, then came back. "I can't remember," he said. "It was on the tip of my tongue, then Dino changed the subject."

"Oh, it's my fault you're sliding into dementia, is it?" Dino responded.

"Just a senior moment," Lance said. "I'll call you back."

Lance didn't call back; Vanessa returned, they finished their dinner, and left.

"Where would you like to sleep tonight?" Stone asked Vanessa, kissing her on the ear.

"Mmmmm, let's see," she said. "There's alone in a cold bed, and there's in your arms. Which should I choose?"

"Home, Fred," Stone said.

When they arrived, he told Fred to just pull up to the front door, instead of them all going in through the garage. They were

73

halfway to the front door when Stone heard a noise and said, "Ricochet!" He ducked to one side of the front stairs, hoping that it was the good side, and freed his Colt .380 from its holster. He whistled loudly at Fred, but he was already pulling into the garage. A moment later Fred was at the garage door, a pistol in his hand.

It had gotten very quiet. "Fred, do you see anything?" Stone called out.

"Nothing, sir, but my night vision hasn't made the adjustment yet."

"Please close the garage door, go into the house, and open the front door from inside," Stone shouted.

"Yes, sir!" The garage door slid shut.

"What's happening?" Vanessa asked.

"Someone took a shot at us — Sorry, at me. He missed."

The front door opened a crack. "All right, sir, I'll cover you from here. When you're ready!"

Stone was ready. He took Vanessa by the hand and, keeping his body between her and the street, ran around the staircase and hurried up the steps. Fred closed the door behind them.

"To answer your question," Vanessa said, "I think I'll sleep here tonight."

12

They lay in each other's arms, panting; the adrenaline produced by the assault had been put to a good purpose.

"How would you like to start your European grand tour in England tomorrow?" Stone asked, after he had caught his breath.

"Anyplace but here would be fine with me," she replied.

"How long will it take you to pack tomorrow morning?"

"An hour," she said. "Half an hour if there are shops at the other end."

Stone called Dino.

"Bacchetti," he said.

"Somebody took a shot at us as we arrived at the house," Stone said.

"Silencer?"

"I didn't hear it, so yes."

"I'll get people on it. Time to flee the country."

"Can you manage tomorrow morning?"

75

"You bet your ass, I can."

"Where's Viv?"

"Singapore. I'll see if she can come home flying west, to England."

"Good. Tell her to arrange some security for us tomorrow at Windward Hall and at the London house, and tell her Mike is welcome, too, if he can take some time off."

"Will do. What time?"

"Faith has to arrange for a second pilot and do her flight planning. Let's say ten o'clock at Jet Aviation."

"That will give me time to make up some story about why I have to go to England," Dino said. "You're on."

Stone hung up.

"It's as easy as that?" Vanessa asked.

"It is if you remember to pack your passport."

"And we don't have to stand in line and get frisked, do we?"

"Nope. I'll frisk you, though, just for the fun of it."

"Oh, good."

The car pulled up to the airplane at 9:45, and Faith and her copilot waited at the bottom of the airstairs. While they and Fred loaded the luggage, Stone and Vanessa walked onto the airplane to find a stewardess waiting for them with a silver tray containing two mimosas. Dino was already aboard. "Viv will meet us in England tomorrow," he said.

By the time they had settled into their seats and fastened their belts, the engines were running. Stone went forward and replaced Faith in the left cockpit seat, and shortly they were at the threshold of runway one. The Gulfstream 500 accelerated down the runway and, with a smooth tug on the sidestick by Stone, took wing. They were off. Stone flew the airplane directly to their assigned cruising altitude, fifty-one thousand feet, then handed the airplane back to Faith and went back to Vanessa.

"I feel safer already," Vanessa said. "Now tell me exactly where we're going."

Stone produced a map of southern England from a side pocket. "Here's London," he said, then moved his finger down the map. "This is the village of Bewley, spelled Beaulieu, this is the Beaulieu River, running down to the Solent, which is the body of water that separates the Isle of Wight, over there, from the mainland." He tapped a spot. "The house is here, on the river."

She inspected the map. "And where do we land? Heathrow? Southampton?"

"We land in my backyard," Stone said.

"During World War II, the RAF built an airfield there, which was not on any air chart and was used for dropping agents of the Special Operations Executive and their equipment and weapons into France and the Low Countries. Two owners after the war took good care of it, and I'm the third."

"How convenient. What do we do about customs?"

"Customs and immigration will drive over from Southampton Airport and meet us, and so will a fuel truck, for the return trip."

"How long are we staying?"

"Until the killer is apprehended or you get sick of the English or the countryside or me, whichever comes first."

"Where are the nearest shops?"

"In London, which is an hour and a half's drive. We can stay at my London house, in Belgravia, which is a stone's throw from Harvey Nick's and Harrods."

"I don't suppose they can bring the dress department over?"

"I'm afraid you'll have to make the effort."

"I can do that."

Lunch, a lobster salad, was served, along with a Cakebread chardonnay. Vanessa was soon out like a light, and Stone moved across the aisle to the seating group where Dino was finishing his lunch.

"I guess you want a report about last night," Dino said.

"I can wait until you've made the lobster disappear."

"Good. That's what I was going to suggest." He finished his lunch at a leisurely pace and accepted another glass of the Cakebread from the stewardess.

Dino stretched his arms and legs. "Okay," he said. "We found where the bullet hit a brick, and that tells us that it wasn't a warning shot; he was trying."

"Oh."

"He missed you by a couple of inches. You were hoping for a warning shot?"

"My name is the last on his list. I had hoped that meant that he'd come after me last."

"Dream on," Dino said. "Did you see a car parked outside the house?"

"There were cars on the other side of the street. I didn't pay much attention to them."

"You should be more observant when somebody is trying to kill you," Dino said.

"I was too busy trying not to get killed."

"A natural reaction, but not helpful to the police."

"Gee, I'm sorry I didn't have time to frisk him and get his driver's license."

"That would be appreciated next time."

79

"You think there'll be a next time?"

"I can't think of a reason why he might stop, can you?"

"No," Stone admitted.

"Question is: When he finds you unavailable next time, will he wait for you to return or just go on killing the others?"

"What's your best guess?" Stone asked.

"I think he'll go after the others. I think he's enjoying himself too much to stop."

"Why?"

"Well, he doesn't have a business reason, does he? Like insurance policies on everybody?"

"I guess not."

"I don't think he's out for revenge. There are too many people on the list."

"Maybe they were mean to him in high school," Stone suggested.

"We thought of that. They all went to different high schools."

"Do you think he travels? Like, to England?"

"Airline tickets are cheap, if you don't mind flying steerage."

"What a comforting thought," Stone said. "Now it's time for my nap." He moved back across the aisle.

13

Major Bugg, the property manager, met them on the ramp with the Range Rover and drove them up, past some cottages, to the main house.

"The pilots and the security people will stay in a couple of the cottages, and here we are at Windward Hall," Stone said. The car came to a stop in front of a large Georgian house, and the staff took charge of distributing the luggage. Stone walked Vanessa around the main floor of the house, finishing up in the study. "Would you like something to drink?" he asked her.

"I'd like to go upstairs and become unconscious right away," she said. "I hate jet lag."

"I'm afraid Gulfstream hasn't quite solved that problem, except we get to choose our takeoff times." He took her upstairs in the elevator to the master suite, where their clothes had been unpacked and put away in their respective dressing rooms.

Vanessa began stripping off clothes, leaving a puddle of them on the bedroom floor, then she kissed Stone and crawled under the covers. Stone was right behind.

They slept straight through until the following morning, when Stone pulled back the curtains and let sunshine pour into the room.

"What's happening?" Vanessa said.

"You have completed your spaceflight and are now on the plant Urg. Enjoy the sunshine. It may not last long."

Vanessa sat up in bed and looked out the window. "Oh, it's beautiful!"

"Didn't I tell you it would be?"

"No."

"I should have, but it could rain at any moment."

As he spoke, it began to rain, hard.

"Is there a little man behind the curtain pulling levers to make that happen?"

"Nature requires no assistance." He looked out the window. "It will stop by the time you're ready for breakfast."

"Do I have to get out of bed?"

"No, I'll have breakfast brought up, that's my usual practice." He picked up the phone and ordered. By the time it had arrived, the sun was out again. Stone checked the radar

82

on his iPhone. "I think that will last the rest of the day," he said.

"I feel wonderfully rested," she said.

"Twelve hours of sleep will do that for you."

"Do you have horses?"

"For plowing or riding?"

"Riding, please."

"I do, but finish your breakfast and digest it for a while first."

Stone looked out the window and saw a Gulfstream 600 turning onto its final approach. "Here comes Viv and Mike Freeman," he said. The two had met up in Singapore, and from there they flew together to England. He called Major Bugg and asked him to have the airplane met and refueled. "I expect they'll stay at least overnight," Stone said to him. "The crew will need to rest." A few minutes later, Bugg called back. "Everyone is tucked in. I don't expect you'll hear from them until dinnertime. I'll let the cook know the numbers."

Stone hung up and finished his breakfast. Vanessa, he noticed, was sound asleep again.

They loped south from the house, across the meadow. "You up for jumping a stone wall?" he asked her. "Or we can go around and take the road."

83

"I'm up for it," she replied.

They sailed over the wall, now on the property of Arrington House, the country hotel that Stone and his French partner, Marcel du Bois, had made from a huge country house. The car park was full, he noticed.

They cantered past the airstrip, now sporting two Gulfstreams, his in the hangar, then down to a bend in the Beaulieu River, where they dismounted. Stone produced lunch from his saddlebag, and they sat down under a tree to smoked salmon sandwiches and half a bottle of champagne.

"I feel wonderful." Vanessa sighed.

"Someone once said, 'Nothing is more exhilarating than having been shot at and missed.' "

"It's a lot better than the alternative, isn't it?" she asked.

"Do you want to go up to London right away, or take a few days here first?"

"I like it here," she said. "Plenty of time for shopping later."

"As you wish."

"Will you fuck me here, please?"

Stone looked up and waved at a passing boat, a few yards away. "I don't think we want to be the entertainment for passing yachtsmen," he said, "but, you may remember, I have a bed."

"Then let's go find it," she said, scrambling to her feet and running for her horse.

14

When Stone and Vanessa came downstairs an hour later, Mike Freeman filled them in on what he'd been trying to tell Stone when their call was cut off. On closer examination of the hit list, he'd recognized the names of many of the victims. More than that, he had a suspect in mind for the killer: an ex–Strategic Services employee named Sig Larkin.

Dino got out his cell phone and made a call to New York. He came back shortly. "Larkin has three arrests," he said, "two bar fights and a domestic violence. He agreed to get counseling for anger management and was released, on his own recognizance. Oh, one other thing: everybody on the list worked at Strategic Services at one time or another."

"I knew I recognized some of the names, though not all," Mike said. "But I remember Sig Larkin."

"Tell me all about Larkin," Stone said.

Mike led the two of them to a sofa. "I'll tell you what I can."

Stone and Dino sat.

"Larkin was hired initially as a security guard on the building staff. He was licensed and had had such experience. Not long after that, our whole security system went blooey, and we didn't have a tech in the building. Larkin looked at it and said he could fix it. He got some tools from his car, and in half an hour had it up and running again. I figured someone who could do that with a very complex system at first sight was wasted as a security guard, so I introduced him to the head of our tech services department, and he hired him as an installer and trained him on our systems. He was a quick study, and in a week or ten days he was making calls to homes and offices where we had installed systems."

"You said he was obstreperous," Stone said.

"Right, he couldn't work with anybody else. Usually, we sent a two-man team, but we started sending him alone. He was all right in dealing with customers, but he didn't like partnering with another tech. He took a swing at a supervisor, and after that, he worked alone."

"How long was he there?"

"Five, six years," Mike said. "Eventually, we decided that we needed somebody in-house full time, so we pulled him off business and house calls and gave him a desk downstairs."

"Would he have met the people on the hit list while doing his work?"

"Sure, he was all over the building."

"Why would he send the list to me? I didn't work in the building."

"No, but you were there a lot — board meetings, visits with me, luncheons, etcetera."

"Buy why am I even on the list?"

"He must have some reason for remembering you unfavorably. Remember, this is a man who takes offense easily. You might have insulted him without even knowing it."

"Anything else about him?"

"Our human resources department had a couple of mild complaints from women about him being handsy, and he was reprimanded twice. The second time, he quit. I never heard from him again."

"How long ago was that?"

"A year, give or take."

"Okay," Dino said. "I'll have my guys run him down and chat with him. We'll want to hear from his wife, too, the one he beat up.

Excuse me." Dino went across the room and starting making calls.

The crews from both airplanes joined them for dinner, so they had a full table. Dino missed the first course but got there in time for the roast beef.

"It's unlike you to be late for eating, Dino," Stone said.

"Well, I got busy with your Mr. Sig Larkin."

"Busy how?"

"Busy like Larkin. He moved out of his apartment a few months ago, owing three months' rent. Funny, he could afford to pay it, but he didn't."

"How do you know he could afford it?"

"Because he won the lottery."

"And he still didn't pay his rent? How much did he win?"

"Oh, not the big-time stuff, but a neighbor said it was something in the range of two million dollars."

"I guess he can afford an airplane ticket, then."

"First class," Dino replied.

"Some people, when they have a windfall, get drunk with power," Mike said. "Think they can get away with anything, because they're rich."

"Gee, I wonder where they get that idea," Dino said.

The crews had returned to their cottages, and everybody else was on cognac and coffee when a dog barked somewhere.

"Your dog is on guard," Mike said.

"I don't have a dog here," Stone replied.

Mike picked up his cell phone and pressed a couple of buttons. "You hear the dog?" he asked. "They don't have a dog. Find out where it's coming from and what it's barking at."

Vanessa was looking uncomfortable. "That's creepy," she said.

"It's better than the dog that didn't bark in the night," Mike replied. "I don't really care who the warning comes from, as long as it comes."

"Mike," Stone said, "I've got a very nice matched pair of 12-gauge shotguns over there in the cabinet. You want to take a walk?"

Mike shook his head. "My people are looking for armed men; we don't want them shooting us."

"Good point," Stone said.

Twenty minutes of silence and acute listening passed, then Mike's phone rang. "Yeah?

90

Good." He hung up. "The dog's owner came home and was greeted noisily."

"Whew!" Vanessa said. "Can I persuade anybody to go to bed with me?"

Stone raised a hand. "I'll volunteer. Good night, everybody. There's more cognac in the cabinet, if you're really thirsty."

Upstairs, Vanessa led him into the room. "Why are the curtain's drawn? It's night."

"Because it's night. Old English tradition, drawing the curtains at dusk. I've always liked dusk. However, there is a point. Until a couple of decades ago, there wasn't a lot of central heating in British houses, so they'd open the drapes to the sun in the morning, then pull them to keep the heat in at night, so they're not entirely crazy."

"I guess not," she said, starting to remove clothing. Stone got done first and propped himself up in bed. "I enjoy watching you get undressed," he said, as she slipped out of her bra.

"I enjoy being enjoyed." She crawled in beside him. "And, as you are aware, I enjoy other things, too."

He searched for the other things.

In the middle of the night, Stone's cell phone rang. He picked it up from the bedside table and checked the caller ID.

91

"Name blocked," it read. He checked the recents; the calling number was blocked, too. Robocall? Probably. Still, he got out of bed and walked naked into the hallway. He stood at the rail and looked downstairs. No lights burning. He looked at the bedroom doors down the hallway: no lights there, either. He took a few deep breaths, then held one and listened. He could hear the big clock near the front door, but nothing between the ticks and the tocks. He exhaled and went back to bed.

He stretched out, and kicked off most of the covers to cool down, and found himself listening hard again. It was awfully quiet in the English countryside, he reflected, as he drifted off.

15

They were having breakfast in bed, and Stone was enjoying the sight of Vanessa's lovely, naked breasts protruding over the tray in her lap.

"I want to go shopping today," she said.

"All right."

"In London."

"Can do. Shall we ask Dino and Viv to join us?"

"How about Mike?"

"He's flying out for New York this morning." He held up a finger and, in the quiet, the big Gulfstream could be heard taking off. "There he goes."

"I'd love to have Viv and Dino along. A girl needs a girlfriend to shop with. You get an instant response that way. And you need a guy to talk with."

"Good point." Stone picked up the house phone and buzzed the butler. "Good morning, Geoffrey," he said. "Would you have the Bentley brought around in an hour, please? And let the Bacchettis know we're going to London for a couple of days. Thank you." He hung up.

"You have a Bentley here, too?"

"Well, there's a Porsche, but the back seat was designed for legless children."

With the women in the rear seat, so they could talk uninterrupted, they set off from Windward Hall at ten o'clock in the Bentley, Stone having told the security chief from Strategic Services their plans. He drove into Beaulieu and made a few turns to give the car behind a view of anyone who might be following them, then took the London road and got onto the motorway.

"There's a noise back here somewhere," Vanessa said from the rear seat.

"What kind of noise?"

"Like wind. I thought the ads say, 'At sixty miles per hour, the loudest noise is the ticking of the clock.' "

"We're doing a hundred and ten," Stone replied.

"Oh."

Dino spoke up. "You're going to get your ass put in a British jail," he said. "Slow down."

Stone brought it down to eighty. "There

94

was a time," he said, "when there was no speed limit on the motorway."

"You can't live in the past," Dino replied.

They drove into Belgravia, to Wilton Crescent, where Stone's house was, then into Wilton Row, the mews behind the house. Stone opened the garage door with the remote, then parked inside. Erskine, the male half of the couple who minded the house, took charge of the luggage, and they went across the mews to the Grenadier, Stone's favorite London pub, and had a light lunch.

Dino looked slowly around the pub. "Mike didn't give us a description of Sig Larkin, did he?"

"No, I don't believe he did."

"Have you got the satellite number?"

Stone produced his iPhone, went to Contacts, and pressed a button. "Hello, Mike."

"Good day, Stone, we're on final approach to Teterboro. Thank you again for your hospitality."

"You're very welcome. Can you give me a description of Sig Larkin?"

"Not really," Mike said. "I remember muscular, but that's all."

"Height? Weight? Hair color?"

"Sorry, he's one of those people who dis-

95

appear into the wallpaper, and apparently, he took the time to scrub his file from our computers before he left. There, we've touched down. Later." Mike hung up.

"Muscular," Stone said.

"That's it?" Dino asked.

"That's it. Very ordinary-looking. He deleted his records at Strategic Services."

"Swell."

They finished lunch and went outside, where Erskine waited with the car. Stone gave Vanessa a house key, closed her car door, and the women drove away.

Stone and Dino had just settled into Stone's study when his cell phone rang.

"Scramble," Lance Cabot said.

"Scrambled."

"You're in London?"

"Spur of the moment."

"Good idea to get out of town. Has Dino made any progress?"

Stone brought him up to date, including a report on Sig Larkin. "Can you see if you have anything on the guy? A description would be helpful."

"Hang," Lance said. Stone could hear the tapping of computer keys.

"Aha," Lance said.

"Aha, what?"

"I've got him. Had to go down a couple of layers. Sigmund Larkin, born NYC, local schools, BA from City College of New York, a year at Fordham Law School, dropped out. Applied to FBI, spent three and a half years as a special agent, terminated 'for cause,' whatever that means."

"What does it usually mean for the FBI?"

"Illegal activity, that sort of thing. I'd have to crack his FBI file to find out more, and they tend to resent that sort of thing. Still, I can take another route. I'll put somebody on it."

"Is there a physical description?"

"Age forty, five-ten, two hundred pounds, sandy hair. There's a photograph."

"Can you e-mail it to me?"

"Okay, done."

Stone contemplated a sandy-haired nobody with indistinct features. "Thanks, Lance, it's useless; probably fifteen, twenty years old."

"We do what we can," Lance said. "Gotta run." He hung up.

Stone showed the photo to Dino.

"You're right, useless," Dino confirmed. "I wonder why we didn't have a photo and that bio."

"Maybe something to do with he used to be FBI?"

97

"Maybe somebody fucked with it."

"Does that happen a lot?"

"No, and neither does no bio and a useless photograph."

"Maybe he has friends in the department."

"Or he's an ace computer hacker. I'll look into that."

Dino switched on the TV and found a cricket match; the game, unaccountably for an American, fascinated him.

"If you're going to do that," Stone said, "I'm taking a nap." He moved to the leather sofa and arranged the cushions. "Let me know if anything at all happens that I should know about."

"Sticky wicket," Dino replied.

"What does that . . . oh, never mind."

"Let me see that photo again," Dino said.

Stone handed him his iPhone.

Dino nodded.

"Why are you nodding?"

"This guy was in the pub when we were having lunch," he said.

"Where? I didn't see him."

"You weren't looking for him. He was at the other end of the bar, drinking a large whisky at midday."

"But . . ."

"It was Larkin."

16

Stone suddenly wasn't sleepy anymore. He got up and peeped through the blinds, into the mews. "Son of a bitch," he said. "He's there."

Dino came over. "Where?"

Stone showed him. "That's the guy. Take a good look at him, and he won't look so ordinary next time."

Stone moved a picture aside, opened his safe and took out a compact 9mm pistol and a spare magazine. "Let's go," he said, and started for the back stairs.

Dino restrained him. "Let's leave this to the pros," he said.

"We're pros," Stone pointed out. "I still have a badge."

"We're not pros to the London constabulary," Dino said. "At least, you're not. Even if we can take him without shooting him or getting shot, we're going to spend the rest of the day answering questions and pulling strings to get out of custody. Call your pros."

Reluctantly, Stone put away the pistol and called the Strategic Services team.

"This is Derek."

"It's Barrington. Larkin is standing in the mews behind my house, about twenty yards from the Grenadier."

"We're on it," the man said, then hung up.

Stone went to the window and peered through the blinds. "He's gone," he said, looking up and down the mews.

Dino came and looked. "What's that place across there where cars are parked?"

"There are a few houses in there; it's a sort of arm of the mews. It has a name, but I don't remember it."

"That's the only place he could have got to that fast," Dino said.

Stone called Derek again and reported the news, then hung up. "I've just remembered," he said.

"Remembered what?"

"There's a sort of tunnel and footpath leading from that alcove to Hyde Park Corner and the Duke of Wellington's house. The duke's officers used the Grenadier as their mess, and they needed a direct route to the house."

"Does Derek know that?" Dino asked.

Stone looked again and saw two men running into the recess. "He does now."

They sat down and Dino turned his attention to the cricket match again.

Twenty minutes later, Derek let himself into the house and came to the study. "He scampered. At Hyde Park corner he could have got a taxi in any direction, or just walked across the street and disappeared into Hyde Park."

Stone handed Derek his iPhone with Larkin's photo. "E-mail this to yourself, and spread it around. Larkin is fifteen or twenty years older and maybe ten pounds heavier, dressed in a dark business suit and necktie, and he still has the beard."

"This could come in useful," Derek said, transferring the photo. "Henceforth, anywhere you're going we enter first and look over the inhabitants." He handed Stone a tiny handheld radio. "This is faster than the phone." He left the room and the house and returned to his duties.

"I wish we'd had the photo sooner," Stone said. "Do you think Derek called the police?"

"I'll take care of that," Dino said, digging out his phone and pressing a button. "Sir John Daring," he said into the phone. "I am Police Commissioner Dino Bacchetti of

New York City." A short pause. "Hello, Sir John, how are you? Very well, thanks. You'll remember my friend Stone Barrington? Yes, we're in London for a few days, and we've just spotted a man on the street who is wanted in New York for two murders. I'm sending you an old photo." They talked for another ten minutes, and then Dino hung up. "Okay, Larkin's photograph is now in every street bobby's phone, and the ports and airports have been informed. With the number of cameras this city has operating, I wouldn't be surprised if they have him within the hour." He went back to his cricket match.

An hour later, Stone said, "Dino, if you were Larkin, what would you be doing right now?"

"Shaving my beard and buying some new clothes," Dino said. "That's if he doesn't have a room near here; then he could just change or hole up."

"That's my bet," Stone said. "It's been more than an hour, and they haven't spotted him on the street."

"Cameras or no, the city is still a haystack, and Larkin is a needle."

Stone paced around for a few minutes. "Let's get out of here," he said.

"Where do you want to go?"

"I'll know it when I see it," Stone replied.

"The girls have the car," Dino pointed out.

"And London still has taxis," Stone said.

They ended up on Savile Row, at Stone's tailor. He had several orders in, so he had a final fitting for some suits and jackets, then asked them to be delivered to Windward Hall.

They walked over to the Burlington Arcade. A miniature mall of elegant shops, then across Picadilly and down to Jermyn Street, where Stone found that his shirt order was ready. He had those sent to Windward Hall, too.

Dino looked around and found himself an elegant silk dressing gown and ordered it without asking the price, which impressed Stone, who normally didn't enjoy shopping with Dino, because he was so cheap and wanted to bargain with everybody.

Dino had his purchase wrapped and put into a shopping bag, and they walked all the way back to the house in Wilton Crescent, arriving at the cocktail hour.

They went into the study, and Stone had a look through the blinds into the mews to see if Sig Larkin was back. To Stone's relief, he was not.

Stone poured them a drink, and Dino

resumed his cricket watching on TV. "Is it the same match?" He asked.

"Who cares?" Dino responded. "It's cricket, isn't it?"

"Undeniably," Stone said. He found a book he had been reading the last time he was at the house, and resumed it.

Stone settled into the sofa and opened the book. He read for a few minutes, then something seemed to reflect a light from the wall he was facing. Sunlight, he reckoned, getting up and adjusting the blinds.

"What's the problem?" Dino asked.

"I was getting a tiny flash in the corner of my eye. Must be reflected sunlight."

"Did it have a color?" Dino asked.

"Green or red, I'm not sure."

Dino shrugged and went back to his cricket match.

The flash came again, disturbing Stone. "I can't read with this little light going off," he said.

"I don't see anything."

"It's infrequent, and I can't tell where it's coming from." Stone returned to his book.

"I see it," Dino said. "It's right there."

"Something inside the heating vent?" Stone asked.

The flash came again. "Got it," Stone said. He stared at the spot as he approached the vent. The flash recurred, and he realized that it was coming from a tiny space between the molding and the floorboards, less than a quarter of an inch, he thought.

"What the hell is that?" Stone asked.

17

Stone and Dino got down on their hands and knees and peered at the tiny space. They were rewarded with a tiny but definite flash, red this time. Stone got a powerful little flashlight from a desk drawer and directed the beam at the space. He had to wait another minute for the flash, and this time, he marked the baseboard with a felt-tipped pen.

"What do you think it is?" Dino asked.

A voice from the doorway caused them both to jump.

"What on earth are you two doing?" Viv asked.

Stone got up, took her elbow, led her to the front door and out onto the stoop.

"What are we doing?" she asked.

"Please call your London office and get a tech team over here. We've got some sort of electronic thing in the wall of my study, so you can't make the call from inside."

Viv produced a cell phone from her purse and made the call, then hung up. "Twenty minutes," she said.

"Where is Vanessa?"

"Upstairs with half a dozen shopping bags."

They went back to the study, and Stone held a finger to his lips when Dino started to speak. "Twenty minutes," he whispered.

Dino shrugged and went back to his cricket match.

Twenty minutes later, Stone answered the front door, then stepped out onto the stoop and closed it behind him.

"What's up, Mr. Barrington?" one of the young men asked.

"We've discovered something electronic in the wall of my study. I'd like you to take a look at it, determine what it is, then see if there are any others in the house."

"Show us where," he said.

Stone led them into the study, motioned for them to kneel, and pointed at the mark he had made, then nodded.

The two men put their cheeks to the floor and waited.

"You may have to wait a minute or two," Stone said.

The team leader looked back at him and gave him a thumbs-up. He took a small meter from his case and set it on the floor next to the spot. Shortly, the needle moved straight up, then returned to zero. He got up and motioned Stone back to the front door, then outside.

"You're right," he said. "You've got an electronic device there that seems to be both receiving and transmitting. We'll take a look around and see if there are others. You go back to the study and resume normal conversation, just not about the device."

Stone did as he was told. Half an hour later the team returned and bent down again. The leader took a needlelike tool from his bag, swept it under the baseboard and came out with a piece of wire. He pulled on that, and a moment later a small, black object revealed itself and flashed.

"I need to get to the breaker box downstairs in the garage," the team leader said.

Stone nodded and watched him disappear into the hallway, then, presumably, down the stairs. He was back in fifteen minutes.

"Okay," he said in his normal voice. "You're all clean. We found five of them scattered around the house."

"I don't suppose there's any way to know how long they've been there," Stone said.

"No way to tell. It's very sophisticated equipment, though. My best guess is that it was done recently, and they had to get out before they could get everything wired."

"Okay," Stone said, "we are, apparently, not using the best possible door locks."

"I'd say you're a notch down from the best, but very good. The Israeli locks are best."

"Do you have them?"

"In our van."

"Please replace mine with those and give me a dozen keys."

"Certainly," the man said. "How long can I have?"

"Whatever it takes."

"I reckon two hours. I can duplicate the keys in the van."

"Go to it," Stone said, and the man did.

When the locks had been changed and the keys distributed, they gathered in the study for drinks and chatted quietly.

"Why are we whispering?" Dino asked at his normal volume.

The others laughed.

Vanessa spoke up. "Did they find one of those devices in our bedroom?" she asked.

"Ah, I'm not sure," Stone replied, though he was certain they had.

"Oh, well," she said.

Dino found the TV's remote control and

turned up the volume on his cricket match.

"We won't have to talk to Dino for a while now," Viv said.

"How long do these matches last?" Vanessa asked.

"Hours," Stone replied.

"Forever," Viv echoed.

The match finally ended and Dino switched to CNN International, instead.

A photograph of a man came onscreen.

"Uh-oh," Dino said.

"What?" Stone asked.

"Quiet!"

"This man," the newsreader said, "an American tourist in London named Mark Wiseman, was shot dead earlier today while he waited at a luxury hotel in Mayfair for the doorman to get him a taxi. His name appeared on a so-called hit list of ten people that was delivered anonymously to a New York lawyer some days ago, along with a warning that the ten would all be murdered. Dr. Mark Wiseman, a dermatologist at New York Hospital, was the third on the list to be killed, all by shooting. He leaves a wife and two grown children."

"I take it this confirms our spotting of Sig Larkin," Dino said.

"Indeed," Stone said.

"So, you're not both crazy?" Vanessa asked.

"At least one of us is not," Stone replied.

There was a long silence. "Where are we meant to be dining this evening?" Viv asked.

"At Le Gavroche," Stone replied. The restaurant was one of only a few in Britain that was rated three stars in the *Michelin Guide*.

Viv got out her phone and left the room briefly. When she came back she said, "I've doubled our security team at the restaurant," she said.

18

When they got out of the Bentley at Le Gavroche, they were sheltered by men with large, black umbrellas, though it was not raining.

Once inside, while Stone was being greeted by the maître d', Derek from Strategic Services approached the group. "We've thoroughly swept the restaurant for weapons," he said, "and as you enter, we've temporarily installed a very sensitive metal detector that picks up any object larger than a pack of cigarettes."

"Turn it off while I walk through," Dino said.

Derek did so, then the others entered the dining room. They were seated at a large table at one end. An enormous floral display had been placed a few feet away, blocking the view of them from most of the room.

"Are the flowers bulletproof?" Vanessa asked.

"Unseen, unshot," Stone said.

"Is that Shakespeare?" Dino asked.

Gun Digest," Stone replied, and ordered a bottle of Veuve Clicquot Grande Dame champagne for the table.

Dino's eyes darted around what they could see of the room.

"Dino," his wife said. "Look at me, and if that's too hard, look at Vanessa."

"I'm just being vigilant," Dino replied.

"You're more fun when you are conversant."

"I don't think I've ever dined under these circumstances," Vanessa said.

"In a French restaurant?" Stone asked.

"In a French restaurant while under the protection of armed guards," she replied.

"Count Dino among them," Viv said. "He's always armed."

"Even on airplanes?"

"I'm an honorary air marshal," Dino said, "and anyway, I hardly ever fly on an airplane that doesn't belong to Stone."

They dined sumptuously, which was the only way available at Le Gavroche, then left the restaurant, again shielded by men with umbrellas, but this time it was actually raining.

"I'm glad we're in an armored car,"

Vanessa said.

"I'm afraid we're not," Stone replied. "I bought this one off the floor at the dealer's in Barclay Square."

"Drive faster," Dino said to the driver.

The garage door was opened with the remote control, the car driven inside, and the doors closed behind them, before they all got out and went upstairs and settled in with coffee and brandy.

"I suggest," Stone said, "that we go back to Windward Hall early tomorrow morning, say seven o'clock."

No one said anything.

"If you're all shopped out," Stone said, just to get their attention. "I don't think Larkin is done in London yet. He lucked out to get two of his victims here at the same time, and I think we're likely to be safer there than here. In London it's too easy to follow us. We can decide tomorrow whether to go on to Paris for a bit or back to New York."

"Breakfast at six?" Viv asked.

"Sounds good to me," Vanessa said, "if I can eat and sleep at the same time."

Dino nodded.

They drove back to Hampshire in the pouring rain in a cloud of road mist from their lead car and their tail, but Stone was still very interested in any car that passed them. Once, he saw a man pass who looked a little like Larkin without a beard, driving a Mercedes station wagon, but the man showed no interest in them.

They dropped the car at the front door of the house and hurried inside, leaving parking and luggage to staff and security men.

Derek came to see him in the study. "It's been pretty much quiet here, with one exception."

"What's the exception?"

Derek took out his iPhone, found a photograph, and showed it to Stone. It was of the nosewheels of the Gulfstream; both were flat. "My people heard nothing; they found this on a routine sweep early this morning. It was probably done last night."

"While we were dining at Le Gavroche?"

"Perhaps."

Stone looked up the number for Gulfstream services and called; it was answered immediately, although it was very early in the morning in Savannah, Georgia, where the factory was located. He reported the loss of both front tires from vandalism and was asked to wait while they checked availability of spares in England. They were found, and he was told that a service truck would arrive with the spares by three PM, and that the work would take two or three hours. Stone thanked them and hung up.

Dino came in and sat down. "You want to go to Paris?"

"Yes, that's fine, but we can't go today. Someone put a bullet into both nosewheels on the airplane. Gulfstream is on the way, so we can leave in the morning, if you like."

"Viv is on board for that," Dino said. "I imagine that Vanessa would be for it."

"We'll assume so, and I'll talk with her."

Stone went upstairs and found her unpacking her purchases. He told her about the nosewheels.

"So much for being safer here," she said.

"How would you like to go to Paris for a few days?"

She gave him a smile. "You talked me into it."

"Then put your new things back into the boxes, and I'll have them stowed on the airplane. You can plunder Paris tomorrow."

They had dinner in the study before a cheerful fire, and turned in early.

"I'm not sleepy yet," Vanessa said. "Whatever will we do with the time?"

They made a game of undressing each

other and spent the time well.

Later, in his arms, she asked, "Where are we staying in Paris?"

"I have a house in Saint-Germain-des-Prés," Stone replied.

"Does this fellow, Larkin, know about it?"

"I doubt it, but I'll have the place gone over before our arrival."

"How long is the flight?"

"An hour. Two hours, door to door, what with Paris traffic."

"How convenient," she said.

Stone called Rick La Rose, the CIA station chief in Paris.

It was late there, but he answered his cell, and they scrambled. Stone gave him a brief summary of their problem so far.

"Well, it's always something with you, isn't it?"

"I'm afraid so."

"Is tomorrow morning soon enough for us to go over the house?"

"Yes, we should be there for lunch, but we can eat out, if you need the time."

"Shouldn't take any longer than that," Rick said.

Stone told him about the bugs in the London house and their nature.

"Maybe you'd better have lunch out," Rick said.

118

19

They lunched in the center of Saint-Germain-des-Prés, at Brasserie Lipp, which was Stone's favorite Paris restaurant. The food was Alsatian, as was the beer, and they all had the choucrute garni, a mix of sliced meats and sausages, with sauerkraut and potatoes. The crowd in the restaurant reminded Stone of the group at Elaine's — now long-lamented, since her death — a mixture of arts, academia, and journalism, with a smattering of showbiz, even if he didn't recognize many of them.

Rick La Rose arrived as they were on dessert. He ordered a beer and was introduced to Vanessa. "Your place is clean of any detritus left by departing bad guys," he said, "electronic or otherwise. We had set a bunch of tiny traps the last time you left, and none of them was tripped."

"It's a relief to know that," Stone said, asking a waiter for the bill. "What's going on in Paris these days?"

"Oh, the usual: Russians, Balkans, and jewel thieves from Marseilles, and not much of those. We could use a little excitement; maybe you've brought some with you."

"We're dealing with only one man," Stone said.

"Yeah, I read in the *International New York Times* about your hit list. I did some research: I guess winning ten million dollars in the lottery made him bold."

"I heard it was two million dollars," Stone said.

"That was a cover story, so he wouldn't be besieged by his relatives. Anyway, he dumped them all and abandoned his house without a trace."

"Smart move, if you've got relatives," Dino said.

"And left three months unpaid rent," Stone added.

"A real prince, huh?"

"Born to the blood."

"I'd like to catch him for you, just for the hell of it," Rick said.

"If we're lucky," Stone said, "he doesn't know we're in Paris. And if we're very lucky, he doesn't know yet that we've left England."

"I read he knocked off an American doctor in London."

"Absolutely true, and he was on the hit list. That's three gone, and nobody's laid a glove on the guy." He pointed this remark in Dino's direction.

Rick fished a photo from his inside pocket. "I ran him through our aging program, and this is its best guess at what he looks like now, sans beard."

Stone looked at the photo. "Even so, he's as close to anonymous as you can get."

"Yeah, he does seem to fade in the light, doesn't he?" Rick said.

Rick finished his beer, Stone paid the bill, and they walked out into the Paris sunshine.

"A van delivered your luggage," Rick said. "We got it inside, and Marie unpacked everything. Good luck on finding your stuff."

They walked back to the mews, and Stone let them in through the human-sized door in the big doors that made the mews private.

"Ooh," Vanessa said, looking down the mews. "This is so . . . *French,* isn't it?"

"It is, indeed," Stone agreed.

"Now," Viv said, "you see why we don't travel, unless it's with Stone."

"A good policy," Vanessa replied.

They were greeted at the door by Marie, the cook/housekeeper, a pretty, well-padded woman of indeterminate age, who showed the guests to their rooms while Stone went into the study and stretched out in a comfortable chair.

A few minutes later, Vanessa came in. "That woman is a genius," she said. "I found every single thing she unpacked for me, and each one was exactly where I would have put it myself. Is she for sale? May I buy her from you?"

"She is not, and you may not," Stone said. "What would you like to do this afternoon?"

"Why, shop, of course. What did you think?"

"I'll arrange a car and driver for you," he said, picking up his phone. He chatted briefly with the car service, then hung up. "They'll be here in half an hour."

She came and made a nest in his lap. "You and everyone around you are so attuned to my needs," she said.

"I'm glad you find us tolerable. By the way, your driver will be more than a driver, and he will be armed. Still, it's up to you to be alert for anyone who pays too much attention to you, unless it is I."

She unbuttoned a couple of buttons on his shirt and bit him lightly on a nipple.

"That's unfair when you're leaving in only half an hour."

"Oh, all right," she said, rebuttoning. "You'll have to wait for my return."

"With bated breath," Stone said, allowing her to dismount and return upstairs.

Dino came in, poured himself a scotch from the little bar, and sat down.

"I'm a little surprised," he said.

"At what?"

"At the fact that we seem to have eluded Larkin, at least for the moment. I'd be willing to bet that he's on the Chunnel train as we speak, headed for Paris."

"Oh, God, I hope not," Stone replied. "Did you notice how quickly and easily he disabled the airplane?"

"I did. I fully expected him to attack before we could get it fixed."

"Tell Viv that Vanessa's going shopping."

"Vanessa brought her up to date. They're both going."

"A pity the French don't follow cricket on TV. You'll have to watch soccer."

"World's most boring game," Dino said. "It would be a much better sport if the field were half as long and the goal twice as wide. How can anybody follow a sport where the final score is so often one-nil? You sit there for four hours, or whatever it is, and they score *once*?"

"I'll bet the stadium sells a hell of a lot of

beer," Stone commented.

The women appeared long enough to say goodbye, then they were off on their spree.

"Quiet, isn't it?" Dino said, after the car had left.

"How do you want to spend your afternoon?" Stone asked.

"I think I'll just read something from your library and wait for something terrible to happen," Dino said. He got up and looked through the shelves, then came back with one.

"What did you find?"

"The autobiography of Elia Kazan," Dino said.

"You'll love it," Stone said.

"You've actually read it?"

"I read it, closed it, then opened it again and started over. That doesn't happen very often."

The doorbell rang.

"You expecting anybody?" Dino asked.

"No, and Maria has gone grocery shopping."

"You first," Dino said. "I'll back you up."

20

Stone walked quietly across the living room and into the entry hall, then peered through the glass top of the front door. A man stood with his back to the door, waiting, a tan leather document case tucked under his arm. Near him was a motorcycle with something in French painted on it, and he was husky in build.

Dino was right behind him. "What do you think?"

"I'm not sure."

"Why don't you let him in while I point a gun at him?" Dino suggested. "It might be a good opportunity to kill him."

"Kill who? That's the problem. Get back, he's going to ring the bell again."

They both jumped back into the living room, just as the bell rang.

"Let's see what he does if nobody answers," Dino said.

Stone's iPhone buzzed in his pocket:

Lance Cabot. They scrambled.

"Did you get the documents?" Lance asked.

"What documents?"

"I sent you some stuff by messenger."

"Describe the messenger."

"He'll be on a motorcycle."

"I'll call you back." Stone pushed Dino behind a curtain, then opened the front door just as the man swung a leg over the motorcycle. "Yes?"

"Delivery," the man said.

"Cover me," Stone said over his shoulder to Dino. He tucked his own weapon into the small of his back and walked outside, since the man was staying on his bike.

"Are you Barrington?"

"I am," Stone replied.

"You got picture ID?"

Stone produced his New York driver's license from his wallet.

"Close enough," the man said, looking at the photo. He opened the document case and put his hand inside. Stone half expected it to come out with a gun in it, but instead, he was handed a clipboard bearing a single sheet of paper. "Sign, please." He handed Stone a pen.

Stone signed. "There you are."

"There I am," the man said, taking a

manila envelope from his case and handing it to Stone. Before Stone could open it and see what was inside, the man had started his motorcycle and turned it back toward the Boulevard Saint-Germaine. He stopped; the big oaken doors were closed.

"How did you get in?" Stone asked.

"A car was coming, and I followed him."

Stone reached inside the front door and pressed a button. The big doors swung open, and the man drove into the street and turned right. Stone closed the doors, then stepped back inside.

Dino was holstering his gun. "Whatcha got?"

"Let's go inside and see," Stone said, leading the way. He went into the study and flopped into his chair, while Dino took the other.

Stone read each sheet and then passed it to Dino. "Looks like there's a file on Larkin in both London and Paris, complete with bad photographs."

"You know," Dino said, perusing the paperwork, "I've seen this guy twice so far, and he could still walk up to me on the street and shoot me, and I wouldn't see him coming."

"It's disconcerting," Stone said.

"That's the word I was looking for."

"So what do these files tell us?"

"That he's accustomed to breaking the law, since he left the FBI, and at least two police forces know it. "Three, if you count mine."

"He seems to like bar fights, Dino, and he's proved it in three cities."

"I'll tell you what else is disconcerting," Stone said. "He's a lot richer than we thought. My thinking was that by the time he'd paid his debts, and spread some of the rest around, he'd have pissed away just about all of it."

"But not if he won ten million, instead of two," Dino said.

"I mean, he could be staying at the Ritz."

"He would stand out at the Ritz as not being the type to stay at the Ritz," Dino said. "I doubt they'd rent him a room. I wouldn't."

"He needs a better tailor," Stone said, looking at the photographs again.

"Oh, shit," Dino said.

"What?"

"I forgot. The last time we were here I ordered some suits from Charvet. Time for a fitting."

"I'll go with you," Stone said.

Marie returned from her shopping, so they didn't have to lock up. They walked up to the boulevard and hailed a cab.

Dino went upstairs at Charvet for his fitting, and Stone had a look around downstairs, choosing a couple of ties, a sweater, and some silk pocket squares. He took a seat in a waiting area while they were being wrapped and glanced idly at a silent TV set into a shelf for the purpose of keeping people like him from becoming bored. What he saw did not put him to sleep. He got up and found the remote and turned up the sound. It didn't help much; the newsreader spoke French.

Stone beckoned a saleswoman. "Excuse me, could you translate this news report?"

"Of course," she said. "I've already seen it once, a few minutes ago. It seems that someone has murdered a man who delivers packages for a service. They found his motorcycle on the Boulevard Saint-Germain, and they have just located his dead body in a mews in that neighborhood."

Stone found himself looking at his own oaken gates. "Anything else?"

"No, but they'll run it again in a few minutes; it's an all-news channel."

"Thank you, you're very kind."

"Il n'y a pas de quoi," she said. Think nothing of it.

Stone turned down the volume, set down the remote, and fell back into his chair, digging out his phone.

"Yes?"

"Scramble."

"Scrambled.

"Rick, have you been watching the local television news?"

"No, I only watch that stuff when I'm drunk."

"Less than an hour ago, my doorbell was rung by a man who had arrived by motorcycle. Dino and I were very cautious of him, but he turned out to be a motorcycle messenger delivering some documents from Lance."

"Okay," Rick said, "anything else?"

"I'm at Charvet, and I was watching the news when a report came on that a motorcycle messenger had been murdered. They found his motorcycle nearby, and his body in my mews."

"Here's the question," Rick said. "Was the man you saw the messenger or the man who murdered the messenger?"

That gave Stone pause. "I don't know," he said.

21

Dino got out of the elevator and walked over. "All done. They'll ship my suits to New York."

"Did you, by chance, watch any television while you were waiting?"

"No, I was in a fitting room, no TV. Why? Was there cricket on?"

Stone explained the report to him.

"Where are the girls?" Dino asked.

Stone produced his phone. "Let's find out."

Vanessa answered. "Yes, dear?"

"Where are you?"

"In the car, about to go into Saint Laurent."

"Scrub that and pick us up at Charvet right away." He gave her the address.

"Isn't that a men's store?"

"It is."

"Then why would I want to go there?"

"Don't ask questions, and don't get out of

the car. I'll explain when I see you."

"All right." She hung up.

Stone called Maria and asked her to pack all their things, and told her that someone would pick them up. Then he called Faith, his pilot, and asked her to round up the crew and go to Le Bourget Airport.

"Where should I file for?"

"I'll tell you when I see you," he said. "About an hour." He hung up, called his car service, and asked them to send a van to pick up the luggage and take it to the airplane. He hung up. "What have I forgotten?" he asked Dino.

"Where we're going," Dino replied.

Stone looked at his watch: noon. "Where would this guy have the most trouble following us?"

"Your place in Maine," Dino said without hesitation.

Stone called Faith back. "File for Presque Isle, Maine. We'll clear customs there, then fly to Rockland Airport, then on to Dark Harbor."

"Got it," she said, then hung up.

"Why Presque Isle?" Dino asked. "Isn't that out of the way?"

"Exactly, but not much. The obvious choice is Bangor, but he might think so, too. Presque Isle might add a few minutes to our trip, but clearing is faster. Let's get out of here." They walked out the door, and the car pulled up to the curb. Stone took the shotgun seat. "We're going to Le Bourget, Landmark Aviation. I'll show you the airplane when we get there."

"Are we leaving the country?" Vanessa asked.

"Yes." He told her and Viv what had happened. "Marie is packing our things, and they'll be picked up and taken to the airport."

"Where are we going?" Viv asked.

"My house in Dark Harbor," Stone replied. "That will be the toughest place for him to find us."

"I can't argue with that," Viv said.

When they arrived, Faith and her copilot were conducting their preflight inspection.

"Are we fueled?" Stone asked.

"Topped off," Faith replied. "We'll be finished in about fifteen minutes. Where's your luggage?"

"On the way," Stone said.

As Faith pronounced her inspection complete, a van pulled up, unloaded their luggage, and stowed it.

"We're off," Stone said. While the others were climbing aboard, Stone took the van's driver aside. "Did you notice whether you were followed here?" he asked.

The man shook his head. "No, but I wasn't looking for that." Stone tipped him, then got aboard and closed the door behind him.

"Have you had lunch?" the stewardess asked.

"No."

"The FBO ordered for us. I have sandwiches."

"As soon as we're at altitude," Stone said. The airplane began to move; they were being towed from the hangar onto the tarmac. He went back and took his seat.

"What did the van driver have to say?" Dino asked.

"He saw nothing."

Dino put up his window shade and observed their progress, and Stone did the same. One engine started, then the other. Immediately, they started to taxi.

"What time will we get to Presque Isle?" Dino asked.

Stone checked his watch. "Late afternoon," he said. "Figure half an hour, maybe an hour, on the ground there, while we clear and refuel. We should be in Rockland about five, then we'll fly the Cessna to the island, be there before dark." He sent his caretaker a text with that plan.

"How about the crew?"

"Faith can fly with us, then go back for the crew. They'll be in the guesthouse."

Without stopping, the G-500 turned onto the runway and accelerated. Moments later, they were airborne.

"That's a relief," Dino said, as they banked and turned on course.

The satphone next to Stone rang, and he picked it up.

"It's Rick. I take it you're in flight. Your cell phone didn't work."

"You take it correctly."

"Where are you headed?"

"Presque Isle, Maine, on the Canadian border, where we'll clear, then to my house in Dark Harbor."

"You think he'll follow?"

"If he does, he'll have to fly to Boston, change for Dark Harbor, rent a car, then drive to Lincolnville, where he will have missed the last ferry. And that's only if he can figure out where we're going."

"I approve of your escape plan," Rick said. "I wish I were going with you. It's pretty dull around here."

"Then go help the Paris police capture Sigmund Larkin. That would make my escape plan perfect."

"I'll see what I can do," Rick said. "Bon voyage." He hung up.

Immediately, the satphone rang again, and Stone answered.

"It's Lance. I heard. Where are you?"

"In the air." Stone related his escape plan.

"I'm on the way to Boston as we speak," Lance said. "I'm giving a speech at Harvard. I may drop in on you afterward."

"We'd be glad to have you," Stone said.

"Remember, you encouraged me." Lance hung up.

"Suppose the guy finds us," Dino said. "What's your escape plan then?"

"I don't know. Oh, the yacht, I guess. It's berthed at Rockland."

"A little sea air never hurts," Dino said.

Vanessa spoke up. "Tell me about the house in Maine," she said.

"Don't worry, it'll be a surprise, and you've already got the clothes for it," Stone said.

22

Stone called Joan in New York.

"Yes, sir?"

"We're airborne, en route from Paris to the Maine house, be there sixish."

"Got it."

"Anybody try to kill you?"

"Not yet. I've got my .45 loaded and cocked."

"Good. Let Mike Freeman know where we'll be."

"Will do."

Stone hung up and settled into his comfortable seat, and the stewardess served sandwiches and beer.

"Everything all right?" Stone asked Vanessa.

"Yes, oddly enough."

"Why oddly?"

"Well, since the night I met you I've been poisoned nearly to death, lost my mother, fled the country ahead of a homicidal

137

maniac, and now I'm fleeing France for Maine, a place I've never been."

"I can understand how you might feel a little rattled," Stone said.

"Strangely, I'm perfectly calm, and I'm getting used to following your orders without protest. And, I'm getting nearly all the sex I want."

"There's a bed in the rear compartment, if you'd like to catch up."

"Perhaps a little later," she said. "I'd like a nap right now." She reclined her seat and pulled a cashmere throw over her.

Dino motioned Stone to follow him to a seat a row back. "Listen," he said, "we're going to have to put an end to this."

"I'm all for that," Stone said. "What's your plan?"

"We're going to have to kill the son of a bitch."

Stone blinked. "Just like that?"

"Yeah, and very soon, if possible. Nobody on the planet would fault us for it, let alone arrest us."

"We're not in your jurisdiction, you know," Stone said.

"That's okay, Maine is even better. We have only to satisfy that state cop who runs things there."

"If Larkin were standing here pointing a

gun at us, I wouldn't hesitate, but what you're talking about is pretty cold-blooded."

"No matter what your blood temperature is, the result is the same, isn't it?"

"Not if the result includes prison. I have an aversion to small rooms with bars."

"Am I going to have to do this myself?"

"I wish you would," Stone said. "Anything I can do besides shooting first?"

"I'll work it out and let you know."

"I'd like some notice, but not too much, as that would smack of premeditation."

"Stop thinking like a lawyer and start thinking like a victim."

"I can't help it. I *am* a lawyer, and I'm not a victim yet."

"You're a target, and we can prove it. That's good enough."

"I'll think about that," Stone said. He found himself a throw, stretched out next to Vanessa and let his mind drift.

Stone was awakened by the ringing of the satphone. He rolled over and picked it up. "Hello?"

"Stone, it's Ed Rawls. How you doing?"

"Not too bad, Ed. In fact I'm on my way across the Atlantic to your neck of the woods."

"That's what Joan told me. She gave me

the satphone number, hope you don't mind."

"Not in the least, Ed. What's up?"

"There's somebody prowling around your place."

Stone sat up in his seat. This was impossible. "Tell me more."

"I've seen the guy twice, when I was driving by. He was concealed, but not well enough, and he had a long gun."

"That's not good."

"I read about your hit list in the *Times*. Is this something to do with that?"

"I expect so. We left Paris earlier today. He killed somebody there, but I can't figure out how he could possibly beat us to Dark Harbor."

"You want me to shoot him?"

"I can't ask you to do that, Ed."

"You don't need to ask. It would be my pleasure."

"No, no. Let's wait until we're in residence and discuss it then."

"Okay, Stone, whatever you say."

"Why don't you come to dinner this evening? Dino and Viv are with me, and a girlfriend, Vanessa Baker."

"You talked me into it."

"Drinks about seven?"

"Sure thing. I'll come packing."

140

"Ed, don't shoot some citizen who's just in the wrong place at the wrong time."

"I'll keep my finger off the trigger. See you later." Ed hung up. Rawls was a former CIA officer and station chief who had retired to a cottage near Stone's house, and he knew how to handle himself.

Vanessa stirred. "Did I hear you talk about shooting people?"

"No, you heard me talking about *not* shooting people. That was a friend of mine, a neighbor in Dark Harbor, named Ed Rawls. He's coming to dinner tonight."

They landed at Presque Isle on schedule, cleared in, refueled, and half an hour later, they took off again. Rockland was less than an hour away, and they transferred to Stone's little Cessna 182 and took off for the island, Isleboro — a ten-minute flight to a 2,450-foot runway. Stone's caretaker, Seth Hotchkiss, was waiting for them with his trusty 1938 Ford woodie station wagon. They got in while Seth stowed the luggage, and Faith flew the 182 back for the crew. Seth would come back to the strip for them.

They were settled in, unpacked, and cleaned up by six-thirty and congregated downstairs.

"Drinks on the front porch?" Viv asked.

The front porch was too exposed for relaxed drinking. "It's going to be chilly tonight," Stone said. "Let's have them by the fire, instead." He lit the fire and poured the drinks.

"Tell me about this place," Vanessa said.

"It belonged to my first cousin, Dick Stone, who was CIA. He was poised to become deputy director for operations when he and his wife and daughter were murdered."

"In this house?"

"Yes."

"Where?"

"I'm not going to tell you. Anyway, Dick had put the house into a trust, and he willed me lifetime use of it. I made the trust an offer, and the property was sold to me. Nice thing about it is, because of Dick's rank in the agency, they paid to have the house built to their standards, which included bulletproofing and fireproofing."

"That's comforting."

The doorbell rang.

"That's Ed Rawls," Stone said to the group. "He's joining us for dinner. Stone checked the peephole before letting Rawls in. Ed backed into the room, hand under his jacket, and Stone closed the door behind him.

"He's still out there," Rawls said.

23

Once Rawls was inside, Stone went back to the peephole and checked outside. "I don't see anything moving."

"He's out there, trust me," Rawls said.

"Would a drink relax you?"

"Yes, but without relaxing my vigilance."

Stone handed him a Knob Creek on the rocks.

"I drink this only at your house," Ed said.

"Why not at home?"

"Oh, I suppose I could buy a bottle off the shelf, but this way I associate it with good company, not with getting soused alone."

Dino came and had a look out the peephole, too. "I saw something move," he said.

"Probably a deer, Dino. Larkin could not possibly have beat us here."

"So you don't care who's out there, as long as it isn't Larkin?"

"That's not what I said. If there's somebody lurking, maybe he's a burglar, casing the house, or maybe he's just curious about other peoples' lives."

"A Peeping Tom, you mean."

"Well, yes."

"Can we shoot him for that in Maine?"

"We can't shoot him for that anywhere," Stone replied, "unless he's a threat to our lives."

"He killed a motorcycle deliveryman in Paris this morning," Dino pointed out. "That's enough for me to assume a threat."

"All right, then explain to me how he got here ahead of us."

"He might have chartered an airplane," Dino said. "That's expensive, but he could afford it. He would have cleared at Bangor, which is closer than Presque Isle. That's how he got ahead of us."

"Nah, I don't buy that," Rawls said. "He phoned it in."

"You mean he has an accomplice?" Stone asked.

"Killers sometimes do. Maybe he just called ahead to get the island reconnoitered, but his guy is careless about being seen."

"Now, unlike Dino, you're starting to make sense."

"Then let's drag him in here and beat it out of him."

"Beat what out of him?" Stone asked.

"Whatever he knows," Dino said. "That could help us get ready for Larkin when he shows up."

"Dino's making sense," Rawls said, "but I'm too old to start beating people up, unless they're already bound and gagged. I saw people get beat by guards when I was in prison, and I didn't enjoy it. I can always leave, if you're bound to handle it that way."

"I am not bound that way," Stone said. "Sit by the fire and drink your bourbon."

"Like my pappy told me to do," Rawls said, sinking into a big, leather armchair.

"It reclines, too," Stone said. "There's a handle inside the right arm."

Rawls found the handle, and his feet popped up. "Ah," he said, leaning back, "my favorite piece of exercise equipment."

Stone went to the telephone, looked up the state police number in Augusta, and dialed.

"State police," a young man said.

"Sergeant Young," Stone said.

"It's Captain Young now, sir. Has been for some time."

"Of course. Is he in his office at this hour?"

"No, sir. He wouldn't be, unless it was an emergency. Is it?"

146

"Not yet," Stone said. "My name is Barrington, over on Islesboro, at Dark Harbor. He knows me."

"Yes, sir."

"Could you possibly connect me to him at home?"

"But it's not an emergency?"

"Almost."

"Please hold."

A minute later: "Stone? Tom Young. What's wrong over there? I've been reading about that hit list thing in the papers."

"Even up here?"

"The Associated Press goes everywhere."

Stone explained what had happened so far. "And now we arrive at Dark Harbor, and he's waiting for us — or somebody is. He's been spotted multiple times in the woods around the house, and he's carrying a long gun."

"What would you like me to do? Come and take him away?"

"No, we don't have enough for a charge, except for trespass."

"What, then?"

"I just want you to know that we're feeling threatened. Dino Bacchetti and Ed Rawls are here, and they're both armed."

"So, this conversation is in case somebody shoots the guy, right?"

147

"That's to the point, Tom."

"Well, in your situation, I'd shoot him, if I thought he was threatening my life. If that happens and you do that, I won't put you in jail for it, and I'll get the body hauled away. How's that?"

"All I could ask for," Stone said.

"Just remember, it's a lot of trouble to clean up after a shooting death. It's a lot less trouble if you shoot and miss, and that might scare him off."

"I'll keep that in mind, Tom, and I hope I don't have to disturb you further tonight."

"Write down my home number and cell," Young said, then dictated them to him.

"Got it. Thanks, Tom." Stone hung up.

Rawls was the first to speak. "Okay, do we have official permission to off the bastard now?"

"Not exactly," Stone said, "but if we do that while he's threatening us, Young says he won't arrest us."

"That's good enough for me," Rawls said, getting to his feet and pulling a 9mm pistol from a shoulder holster.

Stone held up a hand. "Now hold on a minute, Ed. If you shoot the guy now, it's going to ruin our dinner, and we don't want that, do we?"

"Well, I guess I can wait until I'm digesting dessert," Rawls replied, holstering his weapon and sitting down again. "But if I see a weapon in his hand after that, he's a dead man."

"Fair enough," Stone said, "and I'm sure Dino will want to help shoot him."

"You betcha," Dino said, raising his drink in salute.

Viv spoke up. "Have you ever seen a more bloodthirsty crowd?" she asked Vanessa.

"Nope," Vanessa replied, "but I'm running when the shooting starts."

"Me, too," Viv replied.

24

They had finished dinner, and Stone was making the rounds with the brandy bottle, when a sound came from outside the house. Everybody's head turned toward the front door.

"What was that?" Viv asked.

Dino was on his feet. "I'm going to find out," he said, pulling his gun and heading that way.

Rawls was right behind him. "Stone? You coming?"

"My gun is upstairs," Stone said, rising. "Be right with you." He got up and started for the stairs. When he was halfway up, he heard the door open and Dino shouting.

"Freeze!" Dino yelled.

Three or four gunshots followed, some louder than the others.

Stone forgot about arming himself and headed for the front door. Dino and Rawls were a dozen strides out, standing over an inert form on the ground, an assault rifle beside him.

"Is he dead?" Stone called from the front porch.

"If he's not, he's wishing he was," Dino replied. "I caught him middle of the chest."

"I didn't even have a chance to fire," Rawls said. "Dino was in the way, but I know that man fired his rifle before Dino shot him."

Stone walked over to the man, who looked to be about six feet tall and heavy. He checked the wrist and neck for a heartbeat. "I can't find a pulse," Stone said. "Dino, you try."

"What for?" Dino asked. "He's shot right through the heart." He poked the man with a foot. "He's dead."

"Okay," Stone said. "You know the drill. Nobody touch him. I'll call Tom Young." He found the cell number and dialed it.

"This is Captain Young," he said. There was a lot of background noise.

"Tom, it's Stone Barrington. Our intruder took a shot at two of us, and he's dead outside."

"I'm on a police boat, halfway there," Young said. "The ferry is through for the day. Give me an hour. I'll come to your dock."

"Thank you, Tom." He hung up and went back into the living room, followed by Dino and Ed.

"I heard you say he's dead," Viv said.

"I did say that," Stone said. "Listen, we're not going to talk about this. It would look as though we were getting our stories straight. Everybody just remember what happened, and keep it to yourself."

"Did he have any identification?" Vanessa asked.

"We haven't searched him. The police will be here in an hour, and they'll do that."

"Can I go look at him?" she asked.

"Yes, but don't touch him or his weapon."

Vanessa went outside and was back in less than a minute. "I think he's dead," she said.

"That's a safe assumption," Stone said, "now change the subject."

Nobody said anything.

Less than an hour had passed when Stone heard the sound of a boat approaching his dock, and a spotlight swept across the living room. He got up and went outside, down to the dock. He took the boat's lines, tied them up, and shook hands with Tom Young. "Come with me," he said.

Young stopped long enough in the living room to be introduced to everybody. "Everybody, sit down, please. I want to hear your accounts of what happened before I take a look at the body." He had brought two state patrolmen with him, and they took people aside, one at a time and questioned them, taking notes.

"We all done with that?" Young asked. "Okay, Stone, where's your corpse?"

Stone opened the front door, led him outside, and looked around. "I don't see him," he said.

Tom and his men joined him and they searched the grounds all the way to the road.

"I thought you said he was dead," Tom said to Stone.

"I checked wrist and throat for a pulse and found nothing," Stone said. "Dino said his shot went right through the man's heart. I don't think he got up and walked away."

They went back into the house.

"Well?" Dino asked.

"He's not there," Stone said.

"Oh? You think he just got to his feet and, with a hop and a skip, walked away?"

"No, I think he had help," Stone said.

"I'm inclined to agree," Young said. "It appears he had an accomplice — or at least a ride. Did you hear any vehicles outside?"

"No," Stone replied, "the house is fairly soundproof when it's buttoned up. A car

153

could have waited on the road while the man approached the house, and we wouldn't have heard it."

"But you all heard a noise outside?" Young asked.

Everybody nodded.

"What sort of a sound?"

"I don't know," Viv replied, "like someone on the front porch."

Everybody else nodded.

Young got out his phone. "Okay, I've got to get some people over here, and we've got to search the island for a vehicle with a corpse in it and make sure it doesn't get on the first ferry at, what, six o'clock?"

"That's right," Rawls said.

Young made his call and hung up. "The local sheriff is bringing half a dozen men. I suggest you all go to bed."

Nobody moved.

"I think we're still dealing with the adrenaline," Stone said. "Would you and your men like beds, Tom?"

"No, I want to be awake when they get here. He said half an hour."

"Would any of you like a brandy?"

"We'd better keep a clear head," Young said.

The sheriff and his men arrived at the dock

in due course. Young gave them his instructions. "Stone, can I borrow your car?"

"There are two in the garage, keys in them. Help yourself." Stone poured himself another brandy and sat down.

Dawn was creeping in when Tom Young returned. "Come with me," he said to Stone, Dino, and Rawls.

They followed him out the door, and he led them to Seth's old station wagon and opened the rear door. "We found him near the ferry," he said. "I guess somebody dumped him." He directed a powerful flashlight at the rear compartment, and everybody got a good look at the body. "Ever seen him before?"

They all shook their heads. "No, but he's a little like the photo we were sent." He took the sheet of paper out of his pocket and handed it to Young, who compared it to the corpse.

"Not him," Young said. "And he has no identification on him."

25

Young and his men stayed for breakfast. "We've dispatched blood samples and prints through the sheriff's office, so we should have the results soon.

"It's troubling that this guy isn't the one who's been killing people," Young said.

"I'll grant you that," Stone said. "It's equally troubling that the dead man had an accomplice — whoever drove the body away. Why do you think he was dumped on the island?"

"Because the other guy knew we'd be searching all vehicles getting on the ferry this morning, and a body would be hard to hide."

The phone rang. Stone answered it and handed it to Tom Young. "The sheriff."

"Morning, Harv. Whataya got for me?" He listened and took notes. "Okay, we'll take the body to Augusta for an autopsy. Thanks for all your help last night." He

156

hung up.

"The guy's name was James Weaver, a former marine. That's why his prints were on record. There was no DNA hit, though."

"Did they get an address for Weaver?"

"No, we'll take care of that."

"Search the Veterans Administration medical records," Stone suggested. "He didn't look all that healthy to me."

Dino spoke up. "That's because he was dead. People generally don't look their best under those circumstances."

"Thank you, Dino, good point."

Young excused himself, and he and his men left for the dock.

"Dino, you want to see what your people can do with James Weaver, ex-marine?"

"Sure," Dino said, and sat down with his phone.

The doorbell rang. Stone checked the peephole before opening it. Lance Cabot stood there, and Stone opened it. "Good morning," Lance said.

"Come in, Lance. Would you like some breakfast?"

"Already had it," Lance replied. "I'd love some strong coffee, though. Did I see uniformed police officers leaving your dock on a boat?"

"State police," Stone said. "We had an

intruder last night, who ended up dead, courtesy of Dino."

Dino gave Lance a little wave from his chair.

"Tell me all of it," Lance said. "Maybe I can help."

Stone told him all of it, and Lance sent an e-mail with James Weaver's name in it. "We cast a wider net than the police departments," he said, sipping his coffee.

Dino hung up. "My office got the same stuff as the Maine guys," he said. "We search the same computer sites."

Lance's phone rang; he stepped away to talk, then came back after a few minutes. "Weaver was black ops for us and the FBI while he was a marine," he said. "Mostly Afghanistan and Iraq, but some domestic stuff for the Feds."

"Maybe that's where he met Sig Larkin," Stone said.

"Right. They were contemporaries at the Bureau."

"Larkin can afford to hire some associates," Stone said.

"Looks as if he did so," Lance said. "And it's my guess that the vehicle driver last night was not Larkin; travel times don't work."

"Just the telephones," Dino said.

"When are you going back to New York?" Lance asked.

Stone looked around. "What about it, people? We're blown here, anyway." Everybody made agreeable noises.

"Today," Stone said to Lance.

"Can I hitch a ride? It's a long hop in the chopper."

"Of course."

"Anyway, I want to see your new airplane."

"Then you shall."

They set down at Teterboro early enough to beat rush hour, cars waited for both Lance and Dino. Stone got their luggage into Dino's car, but Lance waved him over.

"Come ride with me," he said.

Stone got into Lance's Agency SUV, and they left.

"This Weaver's background troubles me," Lance said. "It's one thing having a mad killer running around taking revenge on his former coworkers, but it's another thing to have the work conducted by hardened pros."

"I agree," Stone replied.

"Then I'm going to have some of my people watch over you."

"Work it out with Mike Freeman," Stone said. "We don't want the two groups shooting each other."

"I will do so," Lance said.

"This includes Vanessa?"

"I'll leave her to Strategic Services; hard to justify the expense."

"Fair enough."

They pulled up in front of Stone's house half an hour later, and Stone got out.

"Nice airplane," Lance said.

"Thank you, Lance."

"And thanks for the lift."

"Anytime." Stone went inside through the office door.

"Hey, boss," Joan said, slipping her .45 back into its desk drawer. "Where's the lovely Vanessa?"

"At her lovely apartment. She was homesick."

"You'll be dining in, then?"

"I haven't decided. I'll let you know."

"There's a stack of stuff on your desk."

"I'll unstack it."

"Including one that was delivered by hand."

Stone went into his office, sat down at his desk, and reached for the envelope on top.

Barrington,
 If you're reading this, then you're still

160

alive, but not for long. Jim Weaver was my friend, and he didn't deserve what he got. I'll see that you have time to think about that while you're dying yourself. You have that to look forward to.

Stone didn't know why it wasn't signed, but he wished he could write a retort. He called Vanessa.

"Hey."

"Hey, yourself. I suppose you got back all right. Everything okay there?"

"Not quite, you're not here."

"We'll just have to tough it out," he said. "I don't think either of us should be traveling tonight."

"You have a point."

"Tomorrow night looks good. Dinner here?"

"You're on. I'll see you at the usual time, and I'll bring my toothbrush."

Stone hung up, already looking forward.

26

The following morning Lance called before Stone was out of bed. Lance scrambled, then said, "The news from here is not good."

"What's the news?" Stone asked.

"Sig Larkin had three buddies he served with and worked with later, when he was at the Bureau."

"I guess one of them, James Weaver, is dead."

"Good guess, but not the other two: Clifford Cox and Terence Hardin. Cliff and Terry, to you."

"Why do you think they're involved?"

"Because they were always involved when Larkin had dirty work to do."

"I hope Cox and Hardin are more identifiable than Larkin."

"They are. I've e-mailed you photos, so take a look. See you later." Lance hung up.

Stone went to his e-mail and found the

two attachments. Both photos seemed to have been taken when the two were still on active duty with the marines: they were in uniform and had whitewall haircuts. Cox had a big mustache, while Hardin just wore a sneer. Stone called Lance back, and they scrambled.

"Thanks for the photos," Stone said. "They're what — ten, fifteen years old? You think they still have whitewall haircuts?"

"Sorry about that," Lance said. "They appear to have avoided being photographed since then."

"Are your people on station here yet?"

"They are. There are four of them per shift, and Mike's people have gone home. My people have the photos."

"What caliber are these people?"

"They usually carry .45s," Lance replied.

"I was referring to their brains. Can they wrap them around the age of these shots?"

"We don't hire stupid people," Lance said. "By the way, my guess — and it's only a guess — is that Larkin and his cohorts are sufficiently pissed off about Weaver's death to forget about the rest of the hit list and concentrate on you. So now the hardened pros are *angry* hardened pros. Good luck." He hung up.

Stone hadn't needed to hear that. He got

163

up and took an Alka-Seltzer to keep his breakfast down.

Stone had just sat down at his desk when Dino called. "I've gotta come uptown for an early-afternoon meeting. You want lunch?"

"Sure, but come here; I've had some unpleasant news that makes me not want to be on the street." He hung up without explaining.

Dino turned up on time, and Fred served them clam chowder in the study.

"Okay, so what's the bad news?"

Stone told him about Larkin's cohorts, Cox and Hardin. "Lance says that now they're not just hardened pros, but *angry* hardened pros."

"I see his point," Dino said, "but maybe it's not a bad thing: angry people make mistakes."

"Let's hope so."

"Have you got a long gun in the house?"

"I don't believe in them," Stone said, "but I've got nothing against shotguns with eighteen-and-a-quarter-inch barrels."

"I've got one of those in the car," Dino said.

"I thought you might have."

Dino called his car, and a few minutes later, Joan came upstairs carrying a police riot gun and a box of 12-gauge shells and set them gingerly on the coffee table. "Delivery for you," she said. "Are we expecting a riot?"

"Not really," Stone said.

She left without another word.

"Good choice of weapon," Dino said, "but if you hit anybody with it there'll be a big mess to clean up."

"Yeah, I remember when that guy, Bennedetto, took one in the chest."

"Ah, the Tony Bennedetto case," Dino said, as if remembering it fondly.

"The guys in the police garage wanted to dump his car in the river, rather than clean it up."

"In the end, they used a fire hose," Dino said. "I'll bet it smelled bad the next day, though. I wouldn't want your valuable rugs stained with guts and brains."

"Neither would I."

"And make sure they're not *your* guts and brains," Dino said.

"I'll try to remember that," Stone replied.

Around six o'clock, Stone stationed Fred outside the garage with the door open. When Vanessa showed up in a cab he directed it inside before he opened her door and paid the cabbie.

Stone was waiting for her in the study.

"Do I sense unusual defensive preparations?" Vanessa asked.

"Only a precaution," Stone replied.

"Yeah," she said, "against an early death."

27

Vanessa gave him a kiss, then pointed at the coffee table. "What is *that*?" she asked, indicating the shotgun.

"Oh, that's Dino's. He left it here."

"But not by accident," she said. "It looks like something the police would use."

"Let me get you a drink," Stone said, changing the subject.

"Don't change the subject."

"It's a police shotgun," Stone said.

"Is it a riot gun?"

"Well, if you're quelling a riot, I guess it is."

"Are we anticipating a riot?"

"Vanessa, please; it's just a shotgun."

"Can you put it away somewhere?" she asked.

Stone picked up the gun and put it behind the door. "There, dear, is that better?"

"Yes, now I can pretend it isn't there."

"Whatever works for you," he said, handing her a drink.

They dined on roast chicken, stuffed with sausage, buttered peas, and wild rice, taken with a bottle of Far Niente cabernet.

"We couldn't have done better in a restaurant," she said.

They were on coffee and cognac when Vanessa said, "What's the difference in security between our dining here and out?"

"Exposure, if we dine out," Stone replied.

"Would these people who are trying to kill you hesitate if you were sitting in a restaurant?"

"I expect so. Smart criminals understand that that sort of thing is not in their best interests, because the worse the crime, the harder law enforcement goes after them."

Fred came, took their dishes, and wished them a good evening.

"Are we all alone now?" Vanessa asked.

"We are. Would you like to go upstairs?"

"I don't want to wait that long," she said. "I want your face in my lap now." She pulled him toward her.

"Love to," he said, stripping off her knickers and applying himself to the task at hand. When she had climaxed noisily, they exchanged positions, and it was Stone's turn to be noisy.

Finally, she was curled up, her head on

his chest. She poked at him. "Are you wearing a bulletproof vest?"

"No, I'm not," Stone replied.

"Do you own a bulletproof vest?"

"Yes, from my days as a policeman, but I never wear it."

"Is a bulletproof vest really bulletproof?"

"Some are, some aren't. Most of them would stop a pistol round, but not one from a long rifle."

"Like a hunting rifle?"

"Yes, or an assault weapon, as used by the military."

"Why wouldn't it stop a bullet from one of those?"

"Muzzle velocity," Stone said. "They use longer bullets that hold more gunpowder. Only a big, thick combat vest would stop that kind of round. Is this the kind of after-sex talk you're accustomed to?"

"No, but I have a curious nature. I never miss an opportunity to pick up a little information."

"Are you considering buying a bulletproof vest?" he asked.

"I don't know. Should I?"

"No. I like as little as possible between your breasts and me."

"So, a bulletproof vest would make me Stone-proof?"

"No, it would just take me longer to get at you."

"Let's go upstairs," she said. "And perhaps you should bring the shotgun."

Stone retrieved the weapon and the ammo, and they repaired to the master suite.

"Are your batteries recharged?" she asked, taking off her clothes.

"Gee, I don't know," he replied. "Let's find out."

He was sound asleep when she poked him in the ribs. "Mmmmf," he replied.

She poked him again.

"What?"

"I heard a noise," she said. "Outside the door, I think."

"What kind of noise?" he whispered.

"Like breaking and entering."

He picked up the shotgun, and it felt light; it occurred to him that he had not loaded it. He opened the box of shells and shoved a handful into the weapon, but he didn't rack the slide. "Go into your bathroom and sit in the tub," he said. "Don't turn on any lights." She got out of bed and went into the bathroom. He went to the door and put his ear against it. Nothing. He racked the slide, as a warning to whoever might be on the other side of the door, then he slowly turned the knob and flung open the door, shotgun at the ready, safety off.

There was a night-light at the end of the hallway, and it cast an eerie glow. Stone waited a few seconds, then walked down the hallway, opening the door to two guest rooms and checking them out. Finally, he went back to the bedroom.

"It's okay, you can come out," he called to Vanessa.

She came out of the bathroom. "Why did you tell me to get into the tub?"

"Because it's made of cast iron, and it might stop a bullet."

Then he heard the noise.

"That's it!" she whispered. "That's the noise!"

Stone let out the breath he had been holding and walked to a cupboard on one side of the room. He opened a lower door. "Ice maker," he said. "It replicates the sound of breaking and entering."

She took the shotgun from him and leaned it against the wall. "Well," she said, "we're wide awake now. What can we do to get sleepy again?"

Stone did his duty as he saw it.

His phone rang earlier than it should have.

171

It was Dino.

"Woke you up, didn't I?" Dino asked unapologetically.

"Not quite," Stone replied. "Why?"

"Last night, a woman named Sheila Barton —"

"She's on the hit list."

"I know that; can I tell you what happened?"

"Please do."

"She left her office at six last evening and got into the black car she takes home every night."

"Where does she work?"

"At a security service — not Strategic Services. Smaller."

"And what happened?"

"They had traveled a few blocks, when the car stopped at a traffic light, and a motorcycle carrying two men pulled alongside. The rider rapped on her side rear window with a knuckle, and the second she saw him she hit the deck and started screaming at her driver to get out of there. He acted quickly, ran the light, and the motorcycle followed and got hit by a cab in the cross traffic. The two riders got up and ran, one of them limping, and they were seen to be getting into a gray van and driving away fast."

"Anybody hurt?"

"No, both she and her driver were unscratched. The limper from the motorcycle probably had a minor injury."

"That's good news."

"Today's warning is, watch out for gray vans." Dino hung up.

28

Stone called Dino back.

"Bacchetti."

"What part did your cops play in this incident? They were protecting her, right?"

"After the first few days, she called us and asked us to remove our people, said she felt safe enough."

"Any change in her attitude?"

"We've got two cops on her now."

"Except for me, this is the first time somebody on the list has eluded them, right?"

"Right."

"Maybe it's time to get more aggressive," Stone said.

"Yeah? How do we do that? Shoot first and think about it later?"

"Do this: assign unmarked police cars to drive these people to and from work, and put one cop, besides the driver, in the car with them. Have the guy carry a shotgun, which is more likely to hit the target than a handgun and does less collateral damage, if you're lucky. You can also load them with bird shot instead of buckshot; that will still do a lot of damage at close range while cutting down on the collateral damage. Also, three of those on the list are already dead and don't require further attention from you."

"Six cars and twelve men."

"Your arithmetic is good," Stone said.

"Okay, that's worth a try."

"Now, if you want to get really aggressive, put a couple of motorcycles behind each car, which will give your guys better visibility and they can also give chase more easily."

"Twelve motorcycles and drivers?"

"Yeah, but you can use light motorcycles, not Harleys. They'd be more nimble in traffic. If you want to go cheap, put one motorcycle, not two, on each car."

"What about you?"

"I'm cowering indoors," Stone said. "If I go out and need an escort, I'll call you."

"Your brain works pretty good early in the morning," Dino said, then hung up.

Vanessa wanted to go home and meet her decorator. So, Stone and Fred got her into

175

the Bentley and launched from the garage. No one followed.

Stone went back to his desk and fidgeted. Joan came in. "Cabin fever?"

"You know me too well."

"Can you get out and around without being slaughtered in the street?"

"That remains to be seen." Stone called Dino.

"Bacchetti."

"I'm busting out of here," Stone said. "Send me killer help."

"Where are you going?"

"To be determined. I just have to get out."

"Okay, meet me at La Goulue for lunch at twelve-thirty."

"Done," Stone said. "You book. I want everybody to know I'm lunching with a cop." He hung up and turned to Joan. "Got that?"

"Sure."

"As soon as Fred gets back, tell him we're going out."

"Okay."

"Listen, if you go upstairs to the master bedroom, there's a shotgun leaning against the wall and a box of shells on the bed. Bring them down here, please."

"Right." Joan fled upstairs and returned with the arms, then went to her office.

Stone went into his safe and removed a small 9mm Sig Arms pistol and a shoulder holster and got them on.

Fred walked in.

"Any problems?"

"None at all, sir. I took precautions."

"Then let's get out of here," Stone said. He got into the car in the garage and placed the shotgun on his lap, then Fred rolled out onto the street. Two men on motorcycles, who had been waiting at the curb, followed the car. As they turned onto Park Avenue, Stone noticed a motorcyclist sitting on an idling machine, talking on a cell phone. "See that, Fred?"

"I did, but he's not following us. Where to first, sir?" Fred asked.

"Let's start at Turnbull & Asser," Stone replied. Fred drove him to 50 East Fifty-seventh Street, parked illegally, got out, surveyed the street in every direction, then stood at the rear door of the car with his hand on his pistol while Stone got out and hurried into the store. Fred remained on guard outside, and the two motorcycle cops sat on their machines, watching the traffic.

Stone went up to the third floor and encountered Felix, who looked after the bespoke shirt department. "Yes, Mr. Barrington?"

"Let's see your new swatches," Stone said.

Felix trotted out a couple of thick swatch books, and Stone began to run through them, writing down some fabric numbers on an order form. Stone's back was to the elevator, but he heard it open.

He stood up and reached under his jacket as if he were scratching an itch while he moved to the other side of the table, then watched a woman carrying a large handbag get off the elevator with a small dog on a leash.

Stone went back to the swatch books, this time facing the elevator, while Felix went to see if he could help her. He could not, apparently, and he returned to the table, while she looked at ties.

Stone handed him the completed order form. "Please add four whites — two French-cuffed and two barrel-cuffed. When is delivery?"

"London is running eight weeks right now."

"Good."

A dog barked. Stone looked up to see the woman, who had approached the table, digging into her handbag. Instinctively, his hand went under his jacket, and he loosened the pistol in its holster.

The woman's hand came out of the bag

holding something black, and everything seemed to slow down. Stone didn't wait to identify the object; he yanked the 9mm from its holster and began to swing it toward her, thumbing off the safety. The first round would fire double-action, and he made a mental note to himself to fire a second round, because he was less accurate with double-action. Now he had to wait and either identify the object in her hand or, if he wanted to be sure, fire immediately. On an instinct that had been finely honed to sense trouble, he fired.

The woman, who was not large, flew backward onto the floor in a spray of blood, and the dog began to bark incessantly. Stone didn't need a second shot.

Felix was pressed against a shelf of shirts and yelling something, but Stone was not wearing ear protection, so the shot had rendered him temporarily deaf. He got up and, holding the gun in a firing position, walked toward the supine woman. There was a hole high up in her chest, and coughed-up blood on her lips. Her eyes were wide open, as if shocked or angry: probably both, he reflected.

He reached out with a toe and, without looking directly at it, kicked the black object away from her. "Call 911, Felix," Stone said.

"Tell them that the police are already on the scene, but we need an ambulance. Woman with a gunshot wound to the chest."

Felix found his phone and began calling.

Stone found his own phone and called Fred.

"Yes, sir?"

"Send those two cops up to the third floor right now. You stay there and watch yourself. There's been an attempt. He put the phone away and looked at the woman. She seemed semiconscious, now.

Stone finally found time to take a closer look at the black object on the floor; it was a .22 semiautomatic with a silencer. He began breathing normally again.

29

Dino got out of the elevator, followed by two detectives wearing badges on their breast pockets. The EMTs were working on the woman, doing something to her chest and starting an IV. Dino took a good look at her before they handed him a manila envelope, then wheeled her to the elevator. "How'd it go down?" he asked.

"I was sitting at this table, looking that way." Stone jerked his thumb. "I heard the elevator door open, and I moved over here. She had a large handbag and a small dog on a leash."

"Yeah, the dog's fine. He's downstairs waiting for animal control."

"She put her hand into her bag, groping for something, and I put mine on my gun. I saw her come out with something black, and I made the decision."

"Good thing you didn't think it over," Dino said.

"Yeah, well."

One of the detectives was clearing the .22. "Baretta," he said. "Nice piece, if you're going for the head."

"Anything to add?" Dino asked.

"Nothing," Stone replied.

"Then let's get out of here. I'm hungry."

Dino led the way out of the building to where both their cars were stopped. Dino's SUV had a flashing light going. "Let's take your car," he said. "It's more comfortable." He told his people to follow them, then got into Stone's rear seat.

Stone got in, too.

"You okay?" Dino asked, looking at him closely.

"Yeah, I'm okay. Why not?"

"You ever shoot anybody before? I mean, actually hit them?"

Stone thought about that for a moment. "No."

"Where were you aiming?"

"Center of the chest."

"Good thing for her you're a lousy shot."

Stone didn't argue with that. He'd never spent enough time at the range.

"You missed her heart but knicked a lung, I think. The EMTs were treating her for a collapsed lung."

"Good."

"This is good for us," Dino said. "We get to talk to this one."

"Great."

"There was no wallet or purse inside the big bag, though — no driver's license or credit cards, just some makeup, etcetera. She's likely a pro, but not a great one, or you'd be the one in the meat wagon."

"Yeah, I guess."

"I'm proud of you for shooting first. That's not like you, really."

"I guess it is when my life is at stake," Stone said.

"I guess so. Jeez, I'm hungry."

They pulled up outside La Goulue and waited for the officers to have a look around before they went in and occupied their table.

The waiter brought them their usual drinks, and Dino handed him the menu. "I'll have the steak frites," he said. "Stone?"

"The same," Stone said. "And two glasses of the Côtes-du-Rhône." The waiter headed for the kitchen.

The maître d' came over and shook their hands. "I checked the reservations, Dino," he said. "There's nobody here that I don't know."

"Thanks," Dino said. "Please let us know if a stranger, male or female, comes in."

"Certainly." The man walked away.

Stone excused himself and went into the men's room. He looked at himself in the mirror: a little pale, he thought. He splashed some cold water on his face and neck, wiped it with a towel, took a few deep breaths, then went back to the table.

Dino was on the phone. "Yeah," he was saying, "keep me posted. I want somebody talking to her the minute she's conscious." He hung up. "The woman is in surgery. She'll live, but she won't enjoy it much with the DA breathing down her neck. She'll do time, if she doesn't do some fast talking."

"This is not going to end," Stone said, "until everybody on the list, including me, is dead."

"Unless we get Sig Larkin first," Dino said.

Dino's phone rang. "Bacchetti." He listened. "Thanks, keep calling." He hung up. "The woman had a couple grand in hundreds in her bag," he said. "You're cheap game, apparently."

"That was a down payment," Stone said. "She'd have gotten more if she'd gone home with my scalp."

"Now, there's a pretty thought," Dino said. "You being scalped at Turnbull & Asser."

"I was speaking figuratively," Stone said.

"Yeah, but there was nothing figurative about her," Dino said. "I can't wait until we find out who she is. I'll bet we clear a few more murders."

"There aren't all that many female pros working," Stone said. "I can remember us busting only one."

"Yeah, I remember that one, too. She was some goombah's girlfriend. She was playing a waitress at some joint downtown when these two guys came in. She opened a bottle of wine, and while one of them was tasting it, she put a round in both their heads."

"Who can miss at eighteen inches?" Stone commented.

"Still, it took guts. She was cool."

Their steaks arrived, and Dino dug in.

Stone stared at his, then tried a french fry.

"What's the matter?" Dino asked. "Something wrong with your steak?"

"It's fine, I'm just not hungry." He flagged down a waiter and asked him to wrap up his food.

"Yeah," Dino said. "I guess I'd be off my feed, too, if I'd just shot somebody."

"No, you wouldn't," Stone said. "You'd be halfway through your steak by now."

"You're right, I wouldn't let it come between me and a steak."

Stone sipped a little of his wine. "What do I do next?" he asked.

"I think your suggestions were helpful," Dino said. "We stand a better chance, now."

"Larkin has the advantage, still," Stone pointed out. "We don't know when or where he's coming from next time."

"There's always that," Dino said. "I'll have a quiet word with my people and make sure he takes one in the head."

"Good idea," Stone said.

Dino finished his steak and ordered espresso. Stone stuck with his wine, but not much of it. Dino got the check, and the waiter brought Stone's steak, wrapped to go.

They got up and headed for the door. "Me first," Dino said. "I'll have a good look around."

Stone didn't argue with him.

30

Stone walked into the hospital through the ER door, where he knew one or two people. He snagged a nurse. "Beth, there's a Jane Doe who just got out of surgery. You got a room number?"

"Four oh seven," Beth replied, "but she'll be in the ICU right now. If you're looking to get laid, Stone, she's helpless."

"Gee, thanks." He made his way upstairs and waved his badge at the cop in a chair in the hallway. "Anybody in there with her?" he asked.

"Nope," the cop replied. "They wheeled her into the ICU maybe twenty minutes ago. There's just the nurse on duty."

Stone knew that nurse, too, from when he had been a patient.

"Well, look who's here," she said, smiling.

"Hey, Carol."

"I'll bet you're looking for our Jane Doe, aren't you?"

"You betcha. Is she awake yet?"

"She's stirring; I'll turn up her oxygen a bit." She did so.

Stone pulled up a chair next to the bed and sat down. The woman's eyelids fluttered. She looked to be in her late thirties, probably good-looking when fixed up. He hadn't looked at her face when he had shot her. She opened her eyes and looked at him.

"Mrs. Larkin, I presume. Good afternoon," he said.

Her eyes narrowed.

"I'm told Sig is on his way."

She tried to say something and failed.

He leaned in close. His ears were still ringing from the gunshot. "Yes?"

"Go fuck yourself," she managed to say, then smiled a little.

"Sorry about the bullet in your chest," he said, "but you were trying to put one in mine."

She licked her lips and tried to speak, but failed.

Stone took a glass of water from the side table and fed her the glass straw.

"That's better," she said. "Go fuck yourself."

"I guess you're not accustomed to your victims walking and talking," Stone said.

She smiled again. "Maybe next time."

"Well," he said, "there's not going to be a next time. I expect you're going to do serious time."

"Where's my dog?" she asked softly.

"Oh, he's up at the pound. I expect he'll be adopted before the day's out, he's so cute."

Something like anger wrinkled her face. "He's not for adoption," she said.

"I'm afraid there's no way to establish your ownership," Stone said, "since you won't give a name and an address. That's the minimum required. What's your first name?"

"Frances," she said, to Stone's surprise. "Last name and address? I'll phone the pound."

"Frances Larkin, at . . ."

"Edison Hotel."

"I'm afraid that won't do. They'll need an apartment or a house. Oh, and a phone number, too."

"Where's my bag?"

Stone looked around.

"I'll get it for you," Carol said, then left the room. She brought it back a minute later.

Stone looked inside. "I don't see a phone."

"Side pocket," she said.

Stone found a zippered pocket inside,

189

opened it, and extracted an iPhone. "You want to call Sig?" he asked.

She shook her head.

"I can't look at the contents of your phone without waiting for the police to get a search warrant," Stone said, "unless you want to give me permission."

She shook her head again. "Give it to me."

"I'm afraid I can't do that," Stone said. "You might call a cab and skate on me."

She smiled and shrugged.

"Hope you're not in any pain," Stone said. "The anesthesia will wear off soon. When that happens, let me know, and I'll ask the nurse to get you something."

She nodded.

"What's the dog's name?"

"Trixie."

"Good, the pound will want that. At least he won't have to go through the stress of a name change."

"She," Frances said.

"Sorry, I didn't have time for that inspection. Can I get you anything? A newspaper? A silenced .22?"

"Yes, please."

"Oh, I'm sorry, that's gone to the police lab, and somehow, I don't think you'll get it back. I hope it isn't your favorite piece."

She shrugged.

"Is there anything at all you'd like to talk about?" Stone asked. "I mean, after me there's only your lawyer, and we know how boring lawyers are."

"You're a lawyer," she whispered.

"Yes, but I'm a sweet guy. This is really your last chance to ask for something and, maybe, get it."

"A razor blade," she said.

"Ah, no — then you'd be a danger to yourself or others, as the judges like to put it."

"Just to me."

"I suppose things must look pretty dark, if you're thinking that way. Listen, in my capacity as a lawyer, though not your lawyer, let me give you some free advice. You didn't actually shoot me, so if you're willing to have a real chat, there's a good chance you could walk. In fact, as the intended victim, I can guarantee it. I'll stand up for you in court. After all, you'd be preventing half a dozen more murders. A judge will be impressed."

She said nothing but looked thoughtful.

"Think about it," he said. "What did Sig ever do for you but hang you out to dry? You're not going to hear from him again, you know. You might see him, briefly, before you talk, when he comes to cut your throat.

191

I'm surprised he hasn't already tried."

Stone was conscious of somebody silently entering the room. He cut a glance and saw Dino leaning on the door.

"Tell you what," Stone said. "Give me everything, and I'll continue to offer you free legal advice, informally. I'll get you out and send you on your way with your two grand — and I'll add another five to that."

She looked at him steadily.

"And I'll get Trixie back for you, even if I have to rip her from the arms of some darling child."

This time, she managed a laugh. "I love you," she said, "but go fuck yourself."

Stone laughed, too, and let himself out of the room. He beckoned Carol. "You need to put her on suicide watch. She'll try to off herself if she can figure a way."

"We watch 'em all," Carol said.

"If you'll pay close attention to her, and talk me up, I'll buy you a steak dinner."

"Sure, you will." She snorted.

Stone handed her the bag from La Goulue. "Here's your steak dinner," he said, "in advance."

31

Stone went and sat on a bench in the hallway, next to Dino.

"What did you get?" Dino asked.

"Her first name is Frances," Stone said. "She may be staying, with Larkin, at the Edison Hotel, in the theater district, but don't count on it."

"Anything else?"

"I made her an offer she may not be able to refuse — once she's thought it over."

"You told her she'd walk."

"She didn't actually shoot anybody," Stone replied, "and she probably has a clean sheet. Have you run her prints, yet?"

"Yep. She's got a clean sheet."

"Then give me a chance to work her," Stone said.

"Okay, you've got carte blanche, until I change my mind."

"Good. You can start by sending somebody up to the pound and springing her dog. She'll respond to that."

"What if it's already been adopted?"

"Unadopt it. By the way, it's a girl dog."

"What breed?"

"Uh, small, hairy, cute."

"Color?"

"Brownish, I think."

"You have a photographic memory, don't you?"

"Oh, and her name is Trixie. Maybe she'll be wearing an ID tag with her address on it."

"I guess it's worth a shot." He got on the phone.

Stone was suddenly hungry. He found a nurse, one he didn't know. "Good morning, could you order me some lunch? I'm stuck on the ICU and can't go down to the cafeteria."

She picked up a phone, and in ten minutes Stone was eating some pretty good meatloaf and mashed potatoes.

Dino put his phone away. "How do I get some of that?" he asked.

"You already had a steak."

"I'm hungry again."

"Be nice to a nurse."

Dino tried that and sat down. "Let's hope it works. You were right about the Edison. They were registered under the name Taylor, but they checked out early this morning."

"I don't suppose they left a forwarding address?"

"Sure, Turnbull & Asser."

Dino's lunch came. He tried a bite. "Not bad," he said.

"Not for a second lunch. I'm going to tell on you to Viv."

"Good luck. She's in Budapest."

"You'll gain weight. She'll notice."

"I don't gain weight."

"I hate that about you."

The elevator door opened, and an enormous cop got off, accompanied by a small dog on a leash.

"Trixie!" Stone cried, and the dog ran toward him until she ran out of leash and was left on her hind legs, pawing the air. Stone picked her up and scratched her ears, then her belly. "Hey, Trixie," he said, "I'm your new best friend." He got a big kiss, before he could react.

Dino laughed. "So this is your new interrogator?"

"My accomplice. You don't want to see your mama do time, do you, Trixie?" She barked.

Carol came out of the ICU. "Frances heard that," she said. "You better bring her dog in here, even though it's against all the rules."

"Your patient will recover faster now."

"Yeah, we've seen that work before, just not in the ICU."

Stone got up and carried Trixie inside. Frances's bed was raised a bit more, and she could see them coming.

"Trixie!" she said, as loudly as she could manage.

Stone put the dog on the bed, and she went nuts, making Frances laugh. "You did it," she said. "I thought you were lying, just to get me to talk."

Stone pulled up a chair and sat down. "I haven't lied to you yet, and I'm not going to start now. I can do everything I said I would, and I will."

"I'll walk?"

"You won't do a day after his trial is over."

"Sig can get to me in jail," she said.

"I'll get you into protective custody, in a hotel somewhere, with room service, as soon as you're able to leave the hospital. No one will know where you are but the DA and me."

"I want it in writing."

"You're going to have to trust me. I'm not law enforcement."

"Then I want it from the DA."

196

"After I get it from you, I'll get it in writing from the DA. I won't tell him what you've told me until then."

"I need to take a nap now," Frances said. "We'll talk after that."

"What's your last name?" Stone asked.

"Bowers."

"Okay, get a nap." Stone left her with Trixie curled up next to her.

Stone went back into the hallway and sat down next to Dino. "Her last name is Bowers," he said. "Run that."

Dino got out his phone. "What else has she said?"

"She's tired and needs a nap; I'll stay here, until she wakes up."

"She liked the dog, huh?"

"They have a special bond," Stone said.

"I'll bet."

"Double the guard in the hospital," Stone said. "I want her to wake up alive."

Dino spoke further into the phone. "Done," he said finally. "Frances Bowers doesn't have a record anywhere. I'd say she was a babe in the woods, if she hadn't been carrying that silenced .22."

"There is that," Stone said.

"Did you check Trixie's ID?"

"I forgot, and so did you. I'll do it later."

"You want me to make a list of questions

to ask her?"

"Oh, please! I'll find out what you want to know, but I'll do it my way. I'm not reading her questions from a list."

"Then what are you going to ask her?"

"I'll ask her for her life's story, and believe me, she'll tell me. Everybody likes to talk about themselves. It's talking about Sig that will be tough to get out of her. She's loyal, and she may even love the guy. Go figure."

"He doesn't seem all that lovable," Dino said.

"Of course not, but you're not a woman. Women are capable of loving the most god-awful of men. They can always find something in them to love."

"That's because we're such glorious creatures," Dino said.

"You're not going to get an argument from me on that."

32

Stone dozed on his bench, and sometime later, Carol put a hand on his cheek. "Frances is awake," she said. "And by the way, the steak was delicious, after a minute in the microwave to wake it up."

"You're welcome," Stone said, waking fully and stretching. He drank from the fountain in the hall and flushed the sleep out of his mouth.

"Hello," Frances said, in a voice a little stronger than before. Trixie yapped a welcome, and as soon as Stone sat down next to the bed, the dog jumped into his lap.

"That's amazing," Frances said. "She doesn't usually like men."

"That's because you've been choosing the wrong men. I'm irresistible," Stone said, "as long as you're a dog. Where were you born, Frances?"

"In Ames, Iowa," she said. "My parents both taught at the university there."

"What did they teach?"

"Dad taught the sciences; mother taught English grammar to freshmen who had not mastered it in high school."

"Did you grow up there?"

"I did. Stayed until I graduated college, with a degree in the care and feeding of children. I wanted to open my own day-care center."

"What stopped you?"

"Marriage. To a classmate. He turned out to like making love to men, instead of me."

"Oh, well."

"My attitude exactly. I moved to New York as soon as I had a divorce decree and taught others to do what I had wanted to do."

"Then you met Sig?"

"Right. He was an FBI agent at the time, then he worked for a security company."

"Strategic Services."

"How'd you know?"

"All the people on the hit list worked there at one time or another, except me. I just serve on their board. I have no memory of Sig."

"Well, he remembers you, or you wouldn't be on his list."

"If you should ever hear from him again, ask him: Why me? I'd like to know."

"You snaked a girl away from him, one

who worked there. Sig isn't the forgiving kind."

"When you see Sig, tell him she wasn't worth it."

"You've already told me I'll never see him again."

"You'll see him on one of two occasions," Stone said.

"What are they?"

"In court, or when he comes into this hospital to kill you. Possibly, both."

"Nonsense. Sig would never kill me. He loves me."

"People like Sig don't love anybody, except themselves," Stone said. "That's a hard lesson to learn, but learn it you will."

"You don't know him."

"Thank God for that. Tell me something lovable about him."

She had to think for a while before she spoke. "He remembers birthdays, and that sort of thing."

"So, he has a good memory, especially when it comes to revenge — probably over imagined slights."

"He can be very thoughtful."

"But he used you," Stone pointed out.

"When? How?"

"He sent you to kill me, because he thought he might get caught if he came

201

himself. He thought you were expendable."

"You may have a point there," she said.

"What did he say to you to convince you to do his work?"

She shrugged. "He said no one would suspect a woman."

"What were you supposed to do after you had dispatched me?"

"Take the elevator to the ground floor and walk out, as if nothing had happened."

"Did he tell you to kill Felix, too?"

"Who's Felix?"

"The man who was showing me shirt fabrics."

"Oh, I didn't think about that."

"Sig would have known Felix would call the police. Didn't he mention that to you?"

"It never came up."

"Would you have shot Felix?"

"Certainly not! I didn't have anything against him."

"What did you have against me?"

She thought about that. "You want to kill Sig."

"And how did he convince you of that?"

"He just told me, and I believed him."

"Think about that situation for a moment," Stone said. "Sig, for reasons real or imagined, wants me dead. He was afraid to kill me himself, fearing that he would be killed or, at least, caught, so — unwilling to take that risk for himself — he asked you to risk your life to save his. That was not a selfless act."

"I suppose you're right," she said softly.

She was thinking now, Stone thought. "Do you know what a sociopath is?" he asked her.

"I don't think I have a clear idea about that."

"A sociopath is someone who has no empathy for others. He is the center of his own existence and cares nothing for anyone but himself. He's a person without a conscience."

"You mean he's crazy?"

"No, he has a personality disorder, which prevents him from relating normally to others."

"So, it's not his fault?"

"You'd have to ask a psychiatrist about that," Stone replied. "Sig probably knows what he is, though, and he doesn't care. That's why he would kill you in a nanosecond, in order to protect himself from arrest."

"That's very troubling," she said.

"As well it should be. Do you doubt that Sig could get into this hospital?"

"No, he's very clever, and he still has his

FBI credentials. He reported them lost or stolen when he left the Bureau."

"I don't think he would come in here to rescue you," Stone said. "After all, you're wounded; you couldn't make it to the street. Do you think Sig knows that?"

"I suppose he does," Frances said.

"If you're unwilling to take my advice, what do you think will happen to you when you're released from the hospital?"

"Oh, Sig would help me."

"By that time, Sig will either be in jail or dead," Stone said. "I can tell you what he will do if he comes to trial."

"What would he do?"

"He'll blame you. He'll cook up a story in which you are the villain and he is the victim. Sociopaths always see themselves as victims when things go wrong."

"Trixie, come," she said, and the little dog jumped from Stone's lap onto the bed.

"That is love," Stone said, nodding at Trixie. "That's not what you're getting from Sig Larkin."

"I'm beginning to think that," Frances replied.

33

The nurse, Carol, came back into Frances's room, looking worried.

"What's wrong?" Stone asked.

"A security guard has been found dead at a side entrance to the hospital," she said.

"Uh-oh. Is there a vacant room on this floor?"

"There's a storeroom, two doors down. It's large enough to take the bed."

"Let's go," Stone said, grabbing the bed and motioning for Carol to push the IV stand in one hand and the head of the bed in another.

Stone propped the door open and looked up and down the hallway. The cop on station wasn't on station.

"It's to your left," Carol said, "two doors down."

"What's wrong?" Frances asked.

"Sig is in the building," Stone replied. "Keep Trixie quiet." He pulled the bed, aligned it with the door, and moved it into the hallway, making the turn to the left. He found the storage room door and tried to open it.

"You'll need this," Carol said, tossing him a key.

He unlocked the door and pulled the bed inside, switching on the light.

Carol took something off a shelf and held it up, a doorknob sign reading, morgue pickup. "I'll put this on her door," she said, disappearing down the hall. She came back, rapped on the door, and Stone let her in and closed and locked the door. He looked around at the supplies stacked neatly on steel shelving. He grabbed a sheet, shook it open, and spread it over the bed, covering Frances's face. "Our last line of defense," he said to her. "Keep your breathing shallow."

He found a stool and sat against the wall, the shelving hiding him. "Carol," he said, "go be seen on the floor. If anyone asks you where Frances is, direct them down to the morgue. She died of her injuries."

Carol let herself out of the storeroom and closed the door firmly behind her.

Stone removed his pistol from the shoulder holster, checked that there was a round in the chamber, then thumbed off the safety.

"Please don't shoot him," Frances said from under the sheet.

"Not unless I have to," Stone said. What that really meant to him was, *I'll shoot him if I get the chance.*

Trixie made a grumbling noise.

"Please keep her quiet," Stone said.

He heard rushing feet from the hallway. One man, he reckoned. He heard a door open, then a pause, then the sound of it shutting. He heard a man ask someone, "Where is the morgue?"

Frances heard it, too, and began to move under the sheet. "Sig," she said, as loudly as she could.

Stone pulled back the sheet and clamped a hand over her mouth. "Quiet," he whispered, "or he'll kill you."

She shook her head. He heard the footsteps moving toward the elevator, and a moment later it arrived, and the doors opened and closed. "He's going to the morgue," Stone said, "to make sure you're dead." He took his hand away.

"You don't know him," she said, shaking her head.

"I know him better than you do," Stone said. "He's not the first murderous ex-husband or boyfriend I've dealt with."

"You think everybody is bad," Frances said.

"I think bad people are bad," Stone replied. "I could make a case that you are one of them, but I've come to think better of you."

Trixie seemed to think something was wrong. Stone stroked her head, calming her. "Trixie knows him better than you do," he said to Frances.

Someone rapped at the door. Stone walked over and put his ear against it.

"It's Carol," she said from outside.

Stone opened the door, and Carol flew into the room, propelled by a large man wearing a tweed overcoat and a matching hat.

"Sig!" Frances called out.

"I'm getting you out of here, babe," Sig replied, keeping Carol between himself and Stone.

Stone raised his pistol and fired at Sig's head. His hat flew off, and Stone saw blood on his forehead. He tried to fire again, but Sig had backed out of the room and slammed the door. "It was a scalp wound, not a head wound," Stone said, half to himself.

"Sig!" Frances called again.

"Frances," Stone said, "you might as well

wear a sign around your neck saying, 'Please Shoot Me.' "

Trixie was trembling violently; the gunshot had taxed her eardrums. Stone picked her up and stroked her, saying, "Shhhh." She stopped trembling, and Stone put her back on the bed and got out his cell phone.

"Bacchetti."

"It's Stone. Larkin was just on the fourth floor, looking for Frances. We moved her to the storeroom. He's wearing a tweed overcoat and bleeding from the scalp, where I shot him."

But Dino had hung up. A moment later, Stone heard the elevator open and many feet in the hallway. Someone tried the doorknob, then hammered on the door.

"Stone, it's Dino!"

Stone got the door open.

Dino looked around. "This was a smart move."

"It was a desperate move," Stone said. "He shot a security guard downstairs."

"We're on that," Dino said. "You stay here, until I come back for you. Don't open the door for anybody but me." He left.

"The police will hurt him," Frances said.

"He killed a security guard," Stone said. "They don't hand out lollipops for that."

"He won't hurt me."

"What do you think he's doing here?" Stone asked.

"He'll have an ambulance waiting for me," Frances said.

Stone slapped his forehead. "Of course." He called Dino.

"What?"

"Check to see if there's an ambulance waiting outside. He may be in it."

"Got it." Dino hung up.

Stone went to the window and opened it, letting in traffic noise. He heard a series of pops. "They've flushed him out," he said. The popping stopped, and they could hear an ambulance siren start up, fading as it drove away.

Stone sat down to wait for Dino to return.

34

Twenty minutes later, Stone heard the elevator open, then footsteps. There was a loud rap on the door. "Stone, it's Dino."

Stone unlocked the door and made sure Dino was alone.

"What are you doing?" Dino asked.

"The last person who came through that door had Sig Larkin right behind her."

"And you got a shot at him?"

"Sort of. He was standing behind a nurse that he took with him. I blew his hat off," he said, handing it to Dino, "but I think I only grazed him."

"We found blood all the way out of the building."

"Scalp wounds bleed a lot."

"He got away in an ambulance."

"Figures. Frances, here, thinks he brought the ambulance for her."

"Sweetheart," Dino said to her, "he came here for your blood, nothing else. If Stone hadn't shot him, you'd both be dead now."

She shook her head. "You don't know him."

"Here's what I know," Dino said. "He's murdered a bunch of innocent people in less than two weeks, and he's made multiple attempts at Stone, but Stone is the luckiest guy I know."

"Let's get her back to her room," Stone said.

"We can't go in there right now," Dino said. "Just leave her where she is for a while."

"Is there something in her room that she shouldn't see."

"Yeah. Well, no, now that you mention it. Let's roll her in there."

They got the bed out of the storeroom and turned it into Frances's room. Carol was sitting in a chair next to the window, her throat cut.

"There you go, Frances," Dino said. "Another example of Sig Larkin's tender heart."

Stone plugged in her bed and pressed the button that sat her up. She saw Carol and gave a strangled cry.

"We won't have any more discussions about what a sweet guy Sig is," Stone said. "Carol died trying to protect you from him."

Frances was sobbing now. The crime scene people did their work, then two attendants arrived with a gurney and took Carol's body away. A nurse's aide came in and cleaned up the blood. Dino and Stone each took chairs.

Frances had stopped crying now. "All right," she said. "What do you want to know?"

"Where have you been living?" Stone asked.

"At the Edison Hotel, since all this started."

"Did you know what Sig was doing?"

"Only when I read about it in the papers and saw it on TV. He didn't talk about it in advance."

"Does Sig have an apartment in the city?"

"We moved out of there and into the Edison."

"Where do you think he is now?"

"Looking for another place to live."

"Where do you think he would look?"

"He likes the Upper East Side. He'll look for a short rental, like a month or two."

"Where does he find them?"

"He uses a rental agent named Angela Dunn; she's in the phone book."

"What name would he use with her?"

"Tony Pierce."

213

"Where would he have gone in the ambulance?"

"He'll dump it somewhere."

"What was his long-term plan?"

"He bought a house in Santa Fe, New Mexico, right after he won the lottery, to get away from his family. That's where I met him; I was on vacation there.

"It's on Acequia Madre," she said, and gave him the number.

"I know the neighborhood," Stone said. "It's on the East Side, runs sort of parallel with Canyon Road."

Dino was taking notes.

"How will he travel there?" Stone asked.

"He'll fly, I imagine. He may charter. He's done that before."

"Out of what airport?"

"I don't know." It was the first time she'd said that, and Stone believed her.

"What was his excuse for killing the people on the list?"

"He said they were evil and deserved to die."

"Any details on why he thought that?"

"No, I just took his word for it. Now I see what an idiot I was."

Dino left the room.

Stone sat with Frances until a new nurse was assigned to her, then he took Trixie outside to empty her. On the way back he encountered Dino, who was on the phone.

"Okay," Dino said, hanging up. "We're checking all the airports for charters he might have used. I've talked with the Santa Fe chief of police, and he's staking out the house."

"What's your next move?"

"My next move is, you fly me to Santa Fe."

Stone looked at his watch. "If he has to stop to refuel, we have a shot at beating him there. Let's take your car. Give me a minute." He went back into the room and sat down next to Frances. She had stopped crying but still looked distressed.

"I've got to leave town on business," Stone said. "I'll be gone a day or two. I'll arrange for a secure apartment for you, and you'll be taken there, with a nurse, when the doctor discharges you. All you have to do then is relax and watch old movies on TV."

"I love old movies," she said.

Stone kissed her on the forehead and left. On the way to Teterboro, his first call was to Ed Eagle, a top-notch Santa Fe defense lawyer and an old friend.

"Dino and I are coming your way," Stone said.

"Great! Use my guesthouse."

"Thank you, sold!"

"Will you be here in time for dinner?"

"Maybe, but don't count on us. We'll see you when we see you. I'll call you when we land."

"Okay. I'll let Susannah know."

Stone called Joan and asked her to get Faith to the airplane as soon as possible. "Tell her I'll fly left seat." He asked her to book a rental car in Santa Fe and to pack a bag for him and overnight it to Eagle's address.

In the meantime, Dino was making his own calls and similar arrangements. "I'm good," he said, finally.

They made Teterboro in forty-five minutes, not bad time. The airplane was out of the hangar, and Faith was there with a copilot, preflighting. The fuel truck was pumping JetA.

They got aboard, and Stone went to the cockpit and started to run the checklist. Faith soon secured the outer door and joined him.

"I've already filed," she said. "I'll get the clearance."

Stone started the engines as Faith entered the flight plan and radioed for a clearance to taxi. She got it and Stone taxied.

"Why did you bring a copilot?" Stone asked.

"You only enjoy takeoffs and landings," she said. "You'll want a nap as soon as we're at altitude."

She was right, he knew. He taxied, took off, and got the airplane out of New York airspace, then turned it over to Faith and her copilot and went aft, where Dino was already asleep. It didn't take Stone long to join him.

35

It was getting dark when they set down at Santa Fe, with Stone back at the controls. He cut the engines and called Ed Eagle.

"Hi, there, Stone. Have you landed?"

"We're in, and we've got a rental car. Be with you in half an hour."

"Just in time for dinner. I'll alert the chef." They both hung up.

Stone handed Faith some cash. "Find yourselves a hotel," he said. "I'll call you when we know a departure time." He left them to button down and hangar the airplane.

Ed Eagle lived a few miles north of the city, and his driveway was marked by a huge stone eagle. Stone turned in there and he and Dino handed their luggage to Ed's houseman.

"Come in," Ed said, and he took them to a comfortable study with a cheerful fire

218

burning and the scent of piñion smoke in the air. Ed poured the drinks, and they all relaxed.

"Dinner's in about forty-five minutes," he said. "That's how long it takes a really big porterhouse to grill. Now what's up? This have something to do with that hit list I've been reading about?"

"Everything to do with it, Ed," Stone replied. He brought Eagle up to date on everything that had happened, while Dino checked his messages and made some calls.

"The hospital is discharging Frances Bowers tomorrow morning," Dino said.

"Seems a little early for that, doesn't it?"

"Yeah. I think they just want her out of the hospital before anybody else dies."

"Could be. Can you arrange protective status for her with the DA and find her a decent place with a nurse to convalesce? And ask them to give her cell phone back to her."

Dino started phoning again. By the time they were called to dinner he had a small apartment for her on the East Side, with a spare room for her protectors. "And she's got her phone back," he said.

Susannah Eagle, a semiretired actress who now produced films, most of them shot in

Santa Fe studios, gave the huge steak to Ed to carve, and slices were dished out. The wine was a rare California cabernet, a Screaming Eagle.

"No relation," Ed said.

Dino's phone went off, and he left the table for a couple of minutes, then came back. "There was a light on at Larkin's place, but nobody there. They'll be on it all night and through tomorrow, unless we get word of him somewhere else."

"Then you two ought to get a decent night's sleep," Ed said. "Neither of you looks quite as perky as usual."

"Well," Stone said, "we had two murders and one attempt today. That sort of takes it out of you."

"Especially when the attempt was on Stone," Dino pointed out.

"The attempt was on Frances," Stone said, "I just got in the way."

"Somebody once said that there is no exhilaration like being shot at and missed."

"True," Stone replied, "but that is followed by intense exhaustion and the need for sleep. I passed out on the airplane."

"I heard about the new machine," Ed said. "I'll want a look at her before you take off."

"Better you should think of a tax-deductible reason to fly with us to New York

220

for a few days," Stone said.

"My tax-deductible reason is the theater," Susannah said. "In fact, there's a play I want to see that I might want to option."

"There you are," Stone said.

"I yield to her clarity of thought," Ed replied.

Stone fell asleep to the accompaniment of a coyote's yip and howl; he woke up to birds singing noisily. He showered and dressed and found everybody else in the middle of breakfast, and joined them. That accomplished, he and Dino set out for town.

Stone turned off Paseo de Peralta onto Canyon Road, then took a right. On the next corner was a bookstore with a coffee shop next door, where newspapers were sold.

"Where is Larkin's house?" Dino asked, as they got out of the car.

"Don't look at it, but it's right up the road at my back, on the right. Do you see any cops?"

"No," Dino said. "Thank God."

They went into the coffee shop and bought the *New York Times* and espressos, then took a table at the window, with a view of the parking lot and Acequia Madre.

"What does the name mean?" Dino asked.

"Roughly, 'the mother of all ditches.' An *acequia* is a rainwater-fed ditch that becomes a stream in the rainy season; it often runs across many properties, and the landowners share the water among them. It's managed by an association."

"You could have stopped at 'ditch,'" Dino said.

"But then your education would have been incomplete."

"My education will never be complete, where you're concerned. That's why you talk so much. There's a word for that."

"Articulate?"

"I was thinking of 'verbose.'"

"You wound me."

"Yeah, sure," Dino said. "Can I interrupt you long enough to point out that one of Larkin's black-ops lackeys just walked in here and bought a newspaper?"

Stone forced himself not to look. "Is he buying coffee, too?"

"No, he paid for his paper, and now he's walking out."

Stone got a good look at the man's back as he got into a black SUV. "Why would a grown man have a recruit's haircut?" he wondered aloud.

"To make him easier to follow," Dino said. "Come on."

They tossed down their espressos and made for the parking lot. As they got into their car, the black SUV disappeared up Acequia Madre.

"Drive by at this speed," Dino said. "Don't slow down. I just want to see where the SUV parked.

Stone kept his speed up. "See anything?"

"Most of these houses have gates that are closed."

"Probably have a remote control."

"I didn't see any house numbers."

"People are careless about that," Stone said.

"It's one of three back there," Dino said.

"I expect the cops know which one."

"Let's go back to the coffee shop parking lot."

"Canyon Road is one way. How about a U-turn?"

"I don't want to pass the house twice," Dino said. "Think of something else.

Stone took a left, a right, another left on Alameda, drove back to Canyon Road and to the coffee shop. "What now?"

"I don't know about you," Dino said, "but I'm going to read the *Times*." He unfolded the paper.

36

Stone was taking sections of the *Times* as Dino finished them, then he looked up and saw the black SUV coming down Acequia Madre. Simultaneously, a car on the other side of the parking lot backed out of its space and turned to follow it.

"Okay," Stone said. "Somebody's on the move.

"I saw the unmarked car go after the SUV," Dino said. "Fall in behind it but stay well back."

Stone went out the side entrance of the lot and turned downhill as the police car was disappearing onto Paseo de Peralta. He turned that way, too. Shortly, they were on the road out of town, toward the Opera. They got off at that exit, but turned toward the village of Tesuque, instead. Stone had owned a house there, until he had traded it to the president and her husband for their Georgetown house, where his friend, Holly

Barker, had been living.

As they crossed the little Tesuque River, Stone saw the SUV turn into the parking lot of the Tesuque Market, a grocery and restaurant. "Looks like somebody's having a late breakfast," he said.

"Go past, then come back to within sight of the place," Dino ordered.

Stone complied and parked on the opposite side of the road, a couple hundred yards from the market. "Give me the Arts section, he said. Dino handed it to him. He turned to the crossword, refolded the paper, and started to work it, looking frequently at the market, where the black SUV waited.

An hour later, well after Stone had finished the puzzle, he looked at Dino, who was snoring lightly. "Hey, you," he said.

Dino sat up and looked around. "What?"

"Whoever was in the SUV is taking too long in there. Time for a walk-through."

"You mean me?"

"He knows what I look like, but maybe not you. Just walk in, check out the front porch, then walk in, buy something at the pastry counter and check out the dining room while you're waiting."

Dino got out of the car, crossed the road, and walked down to the market, disappearing inside. A moment later, Dino came out again and waved him over, a paper bag in his hand.

Stone stopped the car, and Dino got in. "What?"

"Neither Larkin nor his henchman is in there. They must have gone out the back door and left in another car."

"We've been sitting here and all the time, they've scampered."

"Maybe not out of reach," Dino said. "The police car is gone, too." He got on the phone said a few words, then hung up.

"They're up the mountain, at a place called 10,000 Waves," he said.

"That's a Japanese-style hot bath and massage place," Stone said, turning left toward Bishops Lodge Road. "We'll take a run up there."

"Wait a minute," Dino said, getting out of the car. He ran back to the front of the market, disappeared, then returned to the car. "I wanted a look inside the SUV," he said. "Clean as a hound's tooth." He opened his paper bag and handed Stone a chunk of carrot cake on a napkin.

Stone continued up the mountain, eating the carrot cake, and his ears began to pop. Twenty minutes later he pulled into the lot at 10,000 Waves. "There's the police car," he said. He parked next to it, and the driver rolled down his window.

"They're up there," he said, pointing up. "They took a hot tub, but they'll have to come back this way. There's nowhere to go once you're up top."

"That's true," Stone said. "I've been there half a dozen times."

"Is there a road up there?" Dino asked.

"What, don't you want to climb five hundred steps?"

"I'm the only person I know who's lazier than you are," Dino replied.

"Well, there is a road up there, used for deliveries." As they watched, a van with the name of a bakery on the side came down that road and turned back toward the main road.

Dino rolled down his window. "One of us ought to follow that truck," he said. "Who?"

"You can have it," the cop replied.

"Let's go," Dino said to Stone.

They backed out and went back to the main road.

"Left or right?" Dino asked.

"The road left dead-ends at the ski resort at the top of the mountain. The right turn takes us back into Santa Fe."

"That way," Dino said.

Stone stepped on it until they caught sight

of the van, half a mile ahead of them. Keeping well back, Stone followed the vehicle through the city to a side street on the other side of town, where it pulled into a lot and parked. One man got out.

"What is that place?" Dino asked.

"It's the bakery," Stone replied. We followed the wrong vehicle."

"Well, shit," Dino said.

Before they could decide what to do, the van started up and backed out of its parking space.

"There's somebody still inside the van," Stone said. "I'm following it."

"Good idea," Dino said, "since we don't have another choice."

The van retraced its steps back to the mountainside, this time driving past 10,000 Waves and on up toward the ski slopes.

"Catch up," Dino said, "you're losing them."

"There's nowhere for them to go, except to the parking lot at the ski slopes."

"I've seen a couple of driveways," Dino said.

"Don't worry. They're trapped." He slowed as they approached the entrance to the slopes. A rail across the entrance to the parking lot told them the place was closed.

"Why would they be closed?" Dino asked.

"You see any snow?"

"No, and I don't see the van, either." They both got out of the car and walked another ten minutes to where they had a clear view of the whole place.

"Absolutely deserted," Dino said.

"Let's go back down the mountain and check out those driveways you saw," Stone said, and they got back into the car and turned around. Stone checked the rearview mirror. "Did you pee in the road back there?"

"I did not," Dino said.

"Then there are only two things that could have made the puddle."

"What are they?"

"Brake fluid or gasoline." The car was doing forty now, and Stone pressed the brake pedal. Nothing. He shifted into neutral, then tried for reverse; the lever wouldn't move. "I think it was both gasoline and brake fluid," he said.

They were doing sixty now, and a very large, very sharp curve was coming up. Dino looked out his window and saw an almost vertical drop into an Aspen forest. "Whatever you do," he said, "don't try to stop on this side of the road."

"Why not?"

"Don't ask."

Stone hung on to the wheel for dear life, as if an iron grip would somehow help. "We're going to have to ditch this car," he said.

"You mean jump out of it?" Dino looked at the speedometer. "We're doing ninety now." He fastened his seat belt and pulled it tight; so did Stone.

"It's either jump or come to a sudden stop," he said. "Like against one of those giant boulders." He looked ahead and saw a car, one going much slower than they. He turned on his flashers and started blowing the horn. The other car was approaching another sharp curve.

"How about against that car?" Dino said. "At least, it's moving. We can use his brakes."

"Look at the bumper sticker," Stone said.

Dino looked and read aloud. "Baby on Board."

37

Stone waited a little too long to make his move. He jerked the wheel to the left, and as he passed the other car he caught a rear fender, knocking the car sideways a bit.

"Didn't you hear me say 'Baby on Board'?" Dino asked.

Stone didn't reply. He was trying to figure out what to do about the giant boulder rushing at them. He aimed his left headlight at it. "Hang on!" he said.

The boulder never moved, but, after colliding, the car went spinning past it sideways, and the airbags popped, blocking Stone's vision for a very important couple of seconds. Then the car rolled onto its side and kept rolling. Stone lost track after the third rollover, then the car came crashing to a rest against an equally large boulder, and Dino seemed to be trying to sit in his lap.

"What are you doing?" Stone asked.

"Breathing," Dino said. "It seemed like a

good idea. Open your door; mine has a boulder holding it shut."

Stone tried his door: jammed solid.

Then someone opened the rear door on Stone's side. "Anybody alive in there?" a man asked.

"One, maybe two," Stone managed to reply.

Then Dino disappeared into the back seat. "I'm out," he called. "Your turn."

Stone worked the lever that changed the position of the seat, then got his heels onto his seat cushion and pushed. Hands grabbed his coat collar and pulled him aft, then out of the car.

"What the hell is the matter with you?" the stranger asked.

"We had no brakes or engine, and I'm afraid I had to use your car to slow us down a little. After that, gravity and the boulders did their work."

"You're lucky to be alive," the man said.

"I'll pay for your damages," Stone said.

"It's a rental," the man replied. He opened the rear seat of his car so they could get in.

"Where's the baby?" Dino asked.

"What baby?"

"There's a sticker on your bumper."

"Belongs to the last renter, I guess."

Stone went back to his car, found his

rental paperwork, then the two of them were introduced to the man and his wife, and they drove down the mountain together. Fortunately, they had rented from the same company.

Stone presented his paperwork at the desk.

"Where's the car?" the clerk asked.

"It became part of the mountain, maybe a mile short of the ski area."

The man looked at his form. "I don't think that's going to work for the company," he said, still looking at the space on the form.

"I think the word you're looking for," Stone said, "is 'totaled.' "

"Ah, yes. That works."

"And I need another car."

"Yeah sure. What would you like?"

"Something heavy, like a Suburban."

"Right."

In fifteen minutes both drivers were on their way in new cars.

"Well," Dino said, "at least they won't be looking for a Suburban." He got on his cell phone again, spoke for a moment, then hung up. "The locals lost them. They weren't in the house, the bakery had reported its van stolen, and Larkin and his buddies are nowhere to be seen."

"What do you want to do?" Stone asked.

"I wonder if there's anything left of that porterhouse from last night?"

"I don't think so. Let's go back to the Tesuque Market and have some green chili stew or a burger."

"Sold," Dino replied.

While they waited for their food, Dino made more calls. "Your girlfriend, Frances, has been moved to a furnished apartment on Third Avenue, in the sixties. There's a nurse on duty 24/7 and two cops sitting on her, so to speak." Dino wrote down the address and phone number on the back of his business card and gave it to Stone. "Visiting hours are whenever you like."

Stone called the number, and the nurse answered. "It's Stone Barrington. May I speak to Frances, please?"

"Hello, Stone?"

"Yes, Frances. How are you feeling?"

"Safer," she replied. "Where are you?"

"In Santa Fe. We think Sig is here, too, but we lost him."

"Did you try his house?"

"Yes. Nobody home."

"Does he know you're looking for him?"

"Yes, I believe he does."

"Well, you know what he does at times like this . . ."

"No, I don't believe you told me."

"He breaks into a house or an apartment and makes himself at home."

"Good to know," Stone said. "Would he have a preference of neighborhood in Santa Fe?"

"As near as possible to his house. He knows the neighborhood."

"Thank you, Frances. Is there anything you need?"

"Dog food, but the cops are out shopping for that."

"Take care. If you think of anything else that might help us, please call. You've got my number."

They hung up. "She had something for you to pass on to the locals," Stone said to Dino. He told him about Larkin's propensity for breaking and entering, and Dino got on the phone.

Their margaritas came, followed in due course by their food.

They had just paid their check when Dino said, "You know, this is the second time Larkin and/or his people have come to this joint."

"I can only remember one," Stone said.

"The second time is right now," Dino said, "and don't look anywhere but at me. One of his heavies is sitting alone at a table in the corner right behind you. He's just started on dessert."

"You recognize him?"

"Why else would I say that? I'm not sure which one he is, but he has the haircut."

"If I can't turn my head, I'll have to take your word for it."

"Here's my plan," Dino said. "You've still got your honorary detective's badge, right?"

"Right."

Dino shifted his body a little to conceal his left side, then he pulled his pistol and held it under the table.

"That's your plan?" Stone asked.

"Here's the rest," Dino said, and began to explain.

38

Stone resisted the temptation to turn his head. "Go ahead, Dino."

"I want you to take out your badge, but not your gun. Go ahead."

Stone reached inside his coat for the badge.

"Left hand," Dino said.

Stone shifted the badge to his left. "Okay, now what?"

"I want you to get up and walk over to his table, staying on his left side. I'll be right behind you, so he won't see my gun."

"Go on."

"You hold up your badge with your left, move more to *his* right, so I can see his right hand, and tell him he's under arrest and not to move."

"Are we going to be legal, here?"

"Who gives a shit?" Dino said. "We're going to take him."

"Okay, ready?"

"I'm ready, and whatever you do, don't move to your right or I'll shoot you."

"I'll try and remember that," Stone said. He stood up, and made a motion of brushing crumbs off his jacket, then he turned and took two steps toward the man's table, sliding to his left. He held up his badge. "Freeze," he said. "You're under arrest." He began reaching under his jacket for his gun.

"Freeze!" Dino shouted from behind him.

Stone had his hand on the butt of his pistol and was tugging on it to free it from the shoulder holster. Whitewall Guy, as Stone had begun to think of him, stood up, grabbed his dessert plate and swung it at Stone's head, making solid, pain-inducing contact.

"I said freeze!" Dino shouted again, then fired a single shot.

That also seemed to have no effect on Whitewall Guy, except to motivate him. He swept his table aside, onto Stone, who was trying to get up, then lowered his head and ran at Dino, who fired again.

Stone finally got to his feet and turned to find Dino had disappeared. Whitewall Guy ran through the restaurant and leapt over the low wall that surrounded the patio out front, then ran to his right, disappearing.

Stone realized he was bleeding from his

right temple. He picked up a fresh napkin from an unoccupied table and held it to his head.

"Will you give me a hand, please?"

Stone looked down and found Dino on his back, then offered him a hand. As he got to his feet they could hear rubber burning on the pavement outside.

"Damn," Dino said, wiping his forehead with his sleeve. That guy ought to be a running back for somebody. I think I hit him twice, though."

Stone turned and looked at the wall behind when the table had sat and saw two bullet holes — one dead center through a painting, the other through the wall next to it. "I don't think you hit him," he said.

"Sit down and stay here," Dino said, then ran out of the restaurant. Stone disregarded his order and followed him, staggering a little.

As he reached the patio, Dino appeared from his right. "Nobody saw the car," he said, then he reached out and caught Stone under his armpits. "I told you to sit down," he said.

Stone sat.

He came to in an ambulance. "You passed out," Dino said helpfully. "Just lie still."

239

Stone lay still and passed out again.

"Just take it easy," a young man in OR green scrubs said, hovering over him. "We're waiting for the on-duty plastic surgeon."

"I didn't come here for plastic surgery," Stone muttered, trying to sit up.

"Your friend insisted on the plastic surgeon. If you don't just lie still, you're going to keep passing out. You've got a concussion. Do you know what you were hit with?"

"A dinner plate," Dino said from behind him.

"That would explain the carrot cake on your forehead," the doctor said.

A young woman entered the room, also in scrubs. "Okay, where's my patient?"

"That would be him," Dino said, apparently pointing.

She examined Stone quickly. "You did the right thing calling me," she said. "That would make a messy scar. I need lidocaine and a syringe," she said to the other doctor, "and a surgical kit." He went away and came back with the items on a tray. She filled the syringe and jabbed Stone's forehead in several places. "It will stop hurting in a moment."

In a moment, it stopped hurting. "Much better," he said.

"All right," she replied, "your job is to remain perfectly still for the next hour, while I make about thirty tiny sutures, so turn to your left a little and get comfortable."

Stone turned his body to the left, and the other doctor tucked a pillow under him to hold him in place.

"I need another pillow under my head, if I'm going to lie still," Stone said, and another, smaller pillow was found.

The surgeon scrubbed up, pulled on some latex gloves, and opened a sealed kit of instruments. "Here we go."

She bent over him and poked him several times. "Any pain?"

"No." Stone realized that he had a nice view of her cleavage and reflected that the sight of breasts was good for morale.

Stone woke in a hospital bed with sunlight filtering through blinds. Dino was asleep in a reclining chair next to the bed.

A nurse carrying a tray came in, shook Dino awake and put the tray in his lap.

"May I have the same, please?" Stone asked.

"Sure. It's a good sign that you're hungry." She left and reappeared with another tray in record time, then adjusted Stone's bed.

"That lady last night did a good job,"

Dino said. "She said most of the repair was under where your hair would usually be, so you won't have much of a visible scar."

"Good," Stone said, starting to eat. "When can we get out of here?"

"The doctor has to see you and discharge you," Dino said. "How do you feel?"

"Pretty good," Stone said. "I guess I had a good night's sleep."

"I can vouch for that," Dino said.

"Any word on Whitewall Guy?"

"Is that his name?"

"It is, until somebody tells me something better," Stone said.

"No sign of him," Dino said.

The plastic surgeon appeared an hour later, this time dressed in a silk blouse and slacks. "How are you feeling?"

"Almost normal," Stone said.

"I'd say you're pretty normal," she replied. "You spent an hour last night looking at my breasts."

"And a pleasant experience it was."

She removed his bandage and inspected her handiwork, then she sprayed the wound with something and applied a fresh bandage.

"Thank you," Stone said.

"Are you married?" she asked.

"Nope."

"Neither am I," she said, placing her business card on his tray table. Stone found his and gave it to her.

"Okay, consider yourself cut loose," she said. "Try not to bump your head on anything and screw up my work."

"I'll do my best," Stone said, watching her leave.

"That bandage will need to be changed in a few hours," she said as she closed the door behind her.

"I don't know why you didn't just screw her right here," Dino said. "Get dressed."

39

Stone was checked out of the hospital at
mid-afternoon and let Dino drive. He got
out his iPhone and began checking his
e-mail. There were a dozen political cam-
paigns' funding requests, it being an election year, and he gave another ten thousand
dollars to Holly Barker's PAC. She was an
old friend and a lover, and she was running
for president, having resigned the office of
secretary of state earlier in the year, in order
to run.

"Holly's looking good in the polls," Dino
said.

"Yeah, I've been following her progress. I
think she'll be okay, barring some gaffe or
accident or new conspiracy theory about
her."

"She'll sail through," Dino said. "You're
the only mistake she's ever made.

"You look kind of funny. Are you going to
pass out again?"

"No, the wound is to my heart," Stone replied.

"Where do you want to go?"

"Someplace restful." As he spoke his phone chimed, signaling a new e-mail. He didn't read it right away. "Any ideas?"

"How about New York City?"

"How about tomorrow morning," Stone suggested.

"All right."

Stone read the e-mail.

This is Jenna Post, your plastic surgeon; I hope you're feeling better. I'd like to change your bandage, so why don't you turn up at my house at sixish, and I will apply the healing arts. Oh, and you can stay for drinks and dinner; I cook.

> Jenna

Her address was at the bottom; it was on Acequia Madre.

Stone replied:

Jenna
I thought, for about half a minute, of playing hard to get, but I changed my mind. See you sixish, and I'll bring the wine and the wound. By the way, I want you to go around your house and lock

245

all the windows and doors, and don't let anybody in, except me. I'll explain later.

He sent the e-mail.

"Dino," he said, "take me to a wine shop."

"Let me guess: the plastic surgeon?"

"She wants to change my bandage."

"Yeah, and your underwear, as well, I bet."

"Right. I need to go back to the Eagles' and change. You can take Ed and Susannah to dinner."

Dino pulled into a parking spot outside a liquor store. "There you go."

Stone went in and bought two bottles of Far Niente, a cabernet and a chardonnay, and a bottle of Knob Creek. Then he went back to the Eagles', changed clothes, and left them a note:

Sorry to miss dinner, but Dino is taking you out. We're leaving the house at nine tomorrow morning to fly back to New York, and we'd love to have you two on board. E-mail me your acceptance.

Then he took the rented Suburban and drove to Acequia Madre. Jenna Post's house was two doors downhill from Sig Larkin's. He parked in her drive, gathered up the booze, and rang her bell.

"Who is it?"

"It's Stone Barrington. You'll recognize me by my bandage."

She buzzed him in, and met him in the front hall. "Ah, yes, that's the correct bandage," she said, taking his hand and leading him into the kitchen.

Stone set his shopping bag on the kitchen island. "I didn't know if you'd want white or red, so I brought both."

"Oh, good. A drink, in the meantime?"

Stone removed the bottle of Knob Creek from the bag and opened it for her. She poured them each a drink.

"Good. Now that you're anesthetized, let me have a look at your wound." She stripped off the bandage, then opened a small black bag that rested on the island.

"You keep a medical kit in the kitchen?"

"It's where most accidents happen," she said. She swabbed the area with alcohol, applied an antibiotic cream and rebandaged it, then she removed a small bottle and a disposable syringe from the bag. "Okay, drop trou," she said.

"This is so sudden," Stone replied, but did as he was told.

She swabbed the area and stabbed him. "More antibiotics," she said. "Infection makes scars, and we wouldn't want that."

"So my ass is safe from infection now?"

"From infection, but nothing else."

Stone hoisted trou and zipped up.

"This is very good whiskey," she said, sipping her bourbon. "Why have I never heard of it?"

"They didn't tell you about good bourbon in medical school?"

"No, we drank only stolen medical alcohol, since it was free."

"This is better, because it's aged in barrels for nine years."

"That would explain it."

"That and the corn. By law, bourbon has to be fifty-one percent corn whiskey."

"Live and learn. Now, tell me why I locked all the windows and doors."

"Because you have a neighbor who's wanted for multiple murders, and he has a habit of breaking and entering."

"Should I move out?"

"No, the police have searched, or are searching, all your neighbors' houses. And I'm here and armed."

"Well, it must be under your jacket. I've already checked out what's under your trousers." She slipped him out of his jacket. "I'd rather you were unarmed," she said, "but not entirely."

She kissed him. "I've been wanting to do

that ever since I saw your ass," she said.

"You don't need an excuse," Stone said, kissing her back.

She stopped. "First, I have to cook." She set about making dinner.

40

Dinner was good, and what came after was even better. "I've wanted to do that," he said, "since I first got a look at your cleavage."

"It's better without the bra, isn't it?"

"Oh, yes." He looked at his watch.

"Oh, do you have to be somewhere?"

"Not right now, but I have to be on an airplane at midmorning."

"An airplane to where?"

"Home, to New York. Here's a thought: Why don't you come with me and stay for a while?"

"You're not joking, are you?"

He pulled her hand down. "Does this feel like I'm joking?"

"One moment, please." She reached for the bedside phone and dialed a number. "Hi, Rex," she said. "Do you think you can hold down the fort for a week or so? I've got the time coming, and I got a nice invitation. You're a prince. You can explain it to the administrator in the morning. Good night." She hung up.

"You're on," she said, "and you certainly feel that way."

They had an encore.

The following morning, she packed, and Stone called Dino and asked him to throw his stuff into his bag.

"The Eagles are coming with us," Dino said.

"Great!"

Stone and Jenna showered together, and she made breakfast, then he drove them to the airport.

"How little is your airplane?" Jenna asked.

"Not too little. You'll be comfortable. Oh, Dino, who you saw at the hospital, will be with us, and the Eagles."

"Susannah Eagle?"

"And Ed."

"I know about them, but we've not met. I'm a huge fan of Susannah's work."

"Be sure and tell her that."

They were buzzed through the gate at the airport; his friends were boarding. Stone turned over the rental car to the lineman and introduced Jenna to the Eagles, and they got aboard. The door was closed, and

251

an engine started turning.

"This is not very little," Jenna said, looking around. "I guess I was thinking of a plane with one engine."

"Those are in my past," Stone said. He adjusted the seating so that they and the Eagles were facing each other, while Dino sat across the aisle.

"What sort of airplane is this?" Jenna asked.

"It's called a Gulfstream 500," Stone replied.

"Will it fly us to New York nonstop?"

"It will fly us to London or Paris nonstop — or would, if we had taken on full fuel, but that would just have added a lot of weight for a flight to New York — or rather, Teterboro, New Jersey, which is the general aviation airport for New York."

"My goodness."

The airplane turned onto the runway without stopping, and shortly they were climbing out and turning east.

"How long a flight?"

"About three hours, depending on the winds."

"How high will we fly?"

"Fifty-one thousand feet, which pilots call flight level five one zero."

"Are we staying at your apartment?"

"At my house," Stone replied

After that, Jenna fell into conversation with Susannah, and she was lost to him. Dino was on the satphone, and Ed was reading an aviation magazine article about the G-500. Finally, Dino hung up, and Stone moved across the aisle, facing him.

"Dino," Stone said, "you look terrible; are you feeling all right?"

"No," Dino replied. "I'm not. I've just learned that there's a leak in my department, somebody fairly high up, I think."

"Do you know who?"

"Not yet, but I'm going to find out." Dino took a deep breath. "I may as well tell you this now: Frances Bowers and her nurse are dead."

"Oh, no, no," Stone managed to say. "What happened?"

"Somebody tased and cuffed the two cops on duty, then took a knife to the two women."

"And you think somebody in your department leaked the location."

"That's about the size of it. Also, they didn't kill the cops, so whoever the leak was apparently made that a condition. Not even the worst guy in the department would have gone along with killing two cops."

"Does the DA know?"

"I just spoke to him. He said we have no case, now. Everything depended on Frances's testimony. I wish we had recorded her."

"I did," Stone said. He turned on his iPhone, found the conversation, and handed it to Dino.

Dino listened. "Can you send this to me and the DA?"

Stone e-mailed the files.

"I feel better now," Dino said. "But you shouldn't."

"I guess not," Stone said. "Don't mention this to the Eagles or to Jenna; it will spoil their trip."

"Okay."

Stone called Joan.

"Yes, boss?"

"We're on the way home, landing in about three hours. Send Fred, and let Mike Freeman know that we need manpower again. I want four people on the house, day and night."

"I'll let Mike know."

"Oh, the Eagles are coming with us, and so is a woman named Jenna Post."

"I take it we'll need only one guest room prepared?"

"Good guess. Listen, you watch yourself, you hear?"

"Are we in trouble again?"

"Yep. I have a feeling I'm next on the hit list."

"I was afraid you were going to say that."

"See you later." He hung up and turned to Dino. "I'm going to have to tell Jenna and the Eagles," he said.

"Okay by me."

"I've ordered people from Strategic Services, but I could use a patrol car outside the house."

"Done," Dino said, and picked up the satphone.

Stone moved back across the aisle. "I have to tell you all something," he said.

Everyone started paying attention.

"Our witness against the hit-list murderer was killed this morning, which means the guy beat us back to New York. I've ordered round-the-clock security at the house, and Dino is going to have a patrol car outside. If anybody wants to go back to Santa Fe, the airplane can turn around right now and take you home."

Nobody said anything. Finally, Ed spoke. "Loan us a couple of handguns. I'd love a shot at this guy."

"Done," Stone said. "Jenna, how do you feel about this?"

"I don't want to go back to Santa Fe, if

this guy is my neighbor," she said. "I think I'd feel safer with you. And the Eagles."

41

Fred met them at the airport and drove them and the Eagles back to Stone's house, while Dino's official car met him and took him to his office.

Joan greeted them at the house, and Fred dealt with their luggage.

"All quiet here?" Stone asked Joan.

"So far. The latest killings have been on the news."

"Yes, and Dino thinks he has a leak in his department."

The moment Dino reached his office he called in his secretary and his deputy. "We've got a leak in the department," he said to them, "probably high up. I want the files of everybody who had any knowledge of the protection of the witness, Frances Bowers, regardless of rank."

"Yes, sir," the secretary said, going to her filing cabinets, while Dino's deputy, Chief

Bill Jenkins, hung back.

"Is there anybody you suspect?" Jenkins asked Dino.

"I've been thinking about it, but I haven't come up with anything. You requisition a couple of investigators from down the ladder and go through every personnel file of anyone who could be involved. Look for recent, large bank deposits, purchase of new cars, houses, etcetera. Let's see if we can pare down the list of suspects."

"My wife was at the supermarket yesterday," Jenkins said, "and she saw Marty Case's wife getting into a new Mercedes." Case was deputy chief of detectives.

"Start there," Dino said. "Find out if the wife has money of her own and which dealer she bought the car from. I want to know if they took out a loan or paid cash."

"I'm on it," Jenkins said, then left. Half an hour later, he returned. "She has no family money, and they paid cash to the Manhattan dealer: $125,000."

"Get Marty up here now," Dino said. "Tell him we need his help on a case and to keep his mouth shut about it. And don't tell the chief of detectives."

Jenkins picked up a phone and made a call. "He's on his way."

Marty Case was shown into Dino's office.

"Have a seat, Marty," Dino said. "I hear you bought a new Mercedes. Congratulations."

Case's shoulders sagged. "I should have known you'd find out."

"Tell us how you paid for a $125,000 car," Dino said.

"I was hoping to keep this quiet," Case said. "Can we keep it in this room?"

"That depends on your answer," Dino said.

"Okay, but if word gets around our lives are going to be hell."

"Why is that?" Dino asked.

"Because I'm going to take a ragging from everybody I work with, and my wife's family are going to be all over us, demanding money. I told her not to buy anything big, and the next day she went out and bought the Mercedes."

"Where'd the money come from, Marty?" Dino asked again.

"My wife hit a number on the lottery," he said.

Dino and Jenkins exchanged a glance.

"How much?" Dino asked.

"A little over three hundred grand net, after taxes."

"You're going to need to substantiate that," Dino said.

Case took a sheet of folded paper from his coat pocket and handed it to Dino, who read it carefully, then handed it to Jenkins. "It's from the New York State Lottery, addressed to his wife."

"Yeah," Case said, "she bought the ticket with money I gave her, but now she says the winnings are all hers, and that she didn't need my permission to buy the car. I may have to sue my own wife. But my guess is, if I do, she'll divorce me."

"New York is an equitable division state," Dino said. "You'll get half the money she says is hers."

"I don't think she's thought that far ahead."

"Then you'd better have a sit-down with her today and take control of the situation."

"Yes, Commissioner, I'll do that," Case said.

"You can go. I want to hear how the meeting works out."

Case left, and Dino and Jenkins burst out laughing.

"I was getting ready to arrest the guy," Jenkins said.

"He's right about what's going to happen, if people find out," Dino said.

The first people from Strategic Services arrived, and Stone showed them the house. While they were at it, they checked every window and door and made sure they were all secure.

Jenna was in Stone's office when he returned.

"I missed my plane," she said.

"That's okay. We've got full-time protection now," Stone said, "and these people are good. Three of the four people Larkin has killed used to work at Strategic Services, so they're taking a keen interest in him."

"I'm delighted to hear that. Is it going to be all right if I do some shopping?"

"Let's wait a day, and see what happens," Stone said. "We'll have the Bacchettis and the Eagles to dinner here this evening, and I have an excellent cook."

"Sounds good," Jenna said. "I'm very impressed with the house. Your card says you're a lawyer; what with the house and the airplane, business must be very good."

Stone laughed. "You're very observant, but I don't rely on my income from the law firm. I was once married to the widow of a movie star — you may remember Vance Calder?"

"Of course."

"She inherited his considerable wealth, and she died a few months after we were married, leaving her estate to our son's trust and to me. I'm a partner in an investment company that manages everything for me, and my net worth has grown substantially since then."

"Ah. I think I remember her death."

"Yes, she was murdered by a former lover. Do you have any murderous former lovers lurking in your background?"

Jenna laughed. "There are lurkers, but not murderous ones, so you can concentrate on Mr. Larkin."

"Fortunately, Dino is in charge of that. He's the police commissioner. He and I were partners when, in my youth, I was an NYPD detective."

"That's very convenient," Jenna said. "With all this" — she waved a hand — "I don't know why you're still single."

"Just lucky, I guess."

"Oh, was the marriage bad?"

"No, it was very good, but since that time, I've stayed lucky."

"Any other marriages?"

"None to speak of. How about you?"

"No, I've been lucky, too."

As she spoke, an alarm went off in the house.

42

There were shouts and the sound of feet on stairs, then a man with a pistol burst into Stone's office.

"Relax," Stone said to Jenna, "he's with us."

"Anybody come in here?" the man asked.

"No," Stone said.

The agent ran out of Stone's office and through the storage room, the exercise room, and the kitchen, to the back door, where he checked the lock, then he turned around and worked his way more slowly along the path he had followed, emerging once again into Stone's office.

"Any luck?" Stone asked him.

The agent shook his head. "It's clear all the way to the garden, and the rear door and windows are secure."

"Then work your way upstairs with the others," Stone said, and the agent left.

"Is it always this exciting around here?" Jenna asked.

"No, the house is normally an island of serenity," Stone replied. He reached for the phone and pressed a button. "Tell you what," he said, "we'll both go shopping. Fred? Get the car ready to leave via the garage. Jenna and I are going shopping."

"Sir," Fred said, "I trust you remember what happened the last time you went shopping."

"I do, and very clearly," Stone replied. "Ten minutes. Go heeled." He hung up.

"Tell me about Fred," Jenna said.

"A French friend gave me a year of Fred's services as a gift. Long before the year was up, I hired him. He is an ex–Royal Marine commando, expert at hand-to-hand combat and the British interservice pistol champion. He and my housekeeper and cook, Helene, are married, and they live in an apartment next door, in a house I now own. Joan lives there, too, and Faith, my pilot."

"I don't think I'll worry while shopping," Jenna said.

Stone looked at his watch. "Do you need anything from upstairs?"

She held up her handbag. "I'm okay."

Stone got a pistol from his safe and secured it in a belt holster, along with a spare magazine, then they went to the garage, where Fred was ready to start the engine. As Stone closed the rear door, Fred opened the garage door with his remote and drove into the street. A cop from the waiting patrol car stood in the street, waving him on, then he returned to his car and followed the Bentley.

"I bought this car from Strategic Services," Stone said. "They have a division that armors vehicles, so this is pretty much bulletproof."

"What a good idea," Jenna said.

"Fred," Stone said, "get us over to the FDR Drive and turn south. Let's see if we're wagging a tail. When we get to the Brooklyn Bridge, do a U-turn and go back to the Upper East Side. Jenna, where do you want to start?"

"How about Bloomingdale's?" she said.

"Fred, you have your instructions. Let the patrol car behind us know what our intentions are."

Fred used a police handheld radio, then went about his business.

Stone called Joan.

"Yes, sir?"

"Let Mike Freeman know we're going to Bloomingdale's. I'd like a male-female team to meet us at the Lexington Avenue entrance and to stick with us for the day. They can ride in the patrol car that will be following us."

"Yes, sir." She hung up.

They arrived at Bloomingdale's, and Stone spotted the Strategic Services team, whom he knew from another occasion.

"Now we are very well cosseted," Stone said to Jenna. He picked out a couple of magazines from the seat pocket in front of them. He needed them, because they were in Bloomingdale's for nearly two hours.

They then spent another hour and a half at Bergdorf-Goodman, and half an hour at a luggage shop on Park Avenue, where, at Stone's insistence, Jenna chose a new set of luggage, as the lone suitcase she had brought with her was inadequate to the task.

Finally, they pulled into Stone's garage, and Fred began unloading and dealing with Jenna's booty.

"Drinks in half an hour," Stone said, "if you'd like to freshen up."

Jenna followed Fred upstairs, like an obedient puppy.

Everyone gathered in Stone's study for drinks, except Dino, who phoned to say he would be late. They were on their second drinks when Dino arrived, looking tired and angry.

"What's wrong, Dino? You look terrible."

"I lost a good man today," Dino said.

"Lost how?"

"By resignation."

"Was he the leak?"

"Very possibly. He was a detective first grade in Homicide, name of Willis Crowder. He had a spotless record."

"Until today?"

"Yes. We went through a process of elimination and interrogated three officers who, though there was no hard evidence, smelled a little hinky to me. Two of them were nervous; Crowder wasn't. He calmly told us that he didn't need a lawyer, and he wasn't going to answer any questions. We got a search warrant and went through his fairly modest apartment in Brooklyn, where we found a safe he wouldn't open for us."

"I assume you brought in a yegg."

"Yep. He had twelve grand in hundreds and a bankbook with a two-hundred-thousand-dollar-plus balance, in his wife's name. He'd apparently been on the take for years. A search of his history told us that he had worked a case with the FBI some years ago, and Sig Larkin was on it, too. After we confronted him with that, Crowder said,

'All I did was save the lives of two cops.' "
He now resides at Rikers Island, and we put
him on suicide watch, to try to keep him
alive long enough to try in a court of law.
The DA is taking it to a grand jury tomorrow."

"You think he'll give up Larkin, if the DA
offers him a sweet deal?"

"I don't know. I suspect that he may be
more afraid of Larkin than of prison. His
nostrils flare every time Larkin is mentioned."

Ed Eagle spoke up. "He'll cave after it
sinks into his skull that he's facing the rest
of his life in prison, if he is."

"He may not be," Dino said. "We have
nothing to connect him to the earlier murders, and he'll probably say that Larkin said
he wanted to free his girlfriend, not murder
her."

"Come on, Dino," Stone managed to say.
"She was pointing a silenced pistol at me."

"Let me put it this way," Eagle said, "in
court, I'd rather be the defense attorney
than the assistant DA prosecuting."

Dinner was served, and they didn't mention Larkin again, for a while.

43

Dinner passed quickly, with much conversation about everything but the matter hanging over them all. Then, Dino's phone rang, and everyone got quiet.

"Bacchetti. Be right there." Dino rose. "Please excuse me, one of my guys wants to see me at the door." He left the room, and took the conviviality with him. Everybody just sat.

Dino came back and sat down. "A search team took Frances's handbag apart and came up with these." He placed a large, zippered plastic bag on the table.

"I see a passport and a wallet," Stone said.

Dino held up a key on a chain. "You missed this," he said. "It's an apartment key — two keys, in fact, and we believe her driver's license may have the correct address on it."

"Have they searched the apartment yet?"

Dino shook his head. "I think somebody

saw that as a gift to me."

"Then let's go," Stone said. He and Eagle stood up; the women seemed to think they weren't invited.

"Ed," Dino said, "are you armed?"

"Courtesy of Stone," Eagle said.

"Leave it here. I can't go around the city with an out-of-stater who's packing."

Eagle thought about that.

"She's not going to shoot you," Dino said. "She's dead."

"Ah," Eagle said and placed Stone's pistol on the table.

"We'll take my car," Dino said. "It's in Stone's garage."

They went down and got into the big SUV.

"May I see her wallet, please, Dino?"

"Sure," Dino said, tossing it to him from the front seat. Keep everything in exactly the same order it's in." He gave the driver an address on East Sixty-sixth Street, and they pulled onto the street.

Stone switched on the overhead light and went carefully through each section of the wallet. There was everything a normal person would carry — driver's license, a health insurance card, three credit cards, a Bloomingdale's charge card. The last thing uncovered was a piece of paper, folded and pressed very flat from being stuffed into the wallet. "Listen to this," Stone said, holding up a sheet of stationery.

To whom it may concern,
   In the event of my death or hospitalization from serious injury or heath issues, please contact Mrs. Terrence Bowers.

"There's an address and phone number in Ames, Iowa," Stone said, then he read on.

On the reverse of this letter are the numbers of accounts at two banks in New York City, each of which has a substantial balance. Mrs. Bower will inherit these accounts, as per my will, which is in her possession. Please see that she knows about these accounts.

"It's signed and notarized," Stone said. "I think Frances understood that, if she stuck with Larkin, bad things might happen to her."

"The hospital would certainly like to see that insurance card," Dino said. "She was admitted an indigent."

Stone returned everything to its original place in the wallet and handed it back to Dino. "Frances said Larkin liked the Upper East Side," Stone said. "Dino, did any of your people talk to that real estate agent who had rented to him?"

"Yeah, and she's promised to call us if she hears from him."

They pulled up in front of the address Dino had given his driver.

"Everybody sit still for a minute, while I have a look around," Dino said. He got out of the car and strolled up one side of the street and down the other, looking at everything, then he got back in. "Okay, here's how it looks. It's a building of only three stories, plus a basement, where there's a light on — probably the super. The two upper floors are dark, as we might expect, since the lessee is deceased and her boyfriend is on the run.

"Dan," Dino said to his driver. "You and one of the guys in the tail car talk to the super. Let him know that we're in the building, and we don't want to be disturbed, and find out everything he knows about Larkin and Frances."

"Yes, sir."

"Ed, Stone, let's go climb some stairs." They got out of the big SUV, went to the front door, and Dino opened it with one of the two keys on the chain. The lights on the stairway came on automatically, and Dino led the way up the steps. At the second

272

floor, he used the other key to open the door. He felt for a light switch and found one. It turned on three lamps in the room. An interior staircase led up to another floor.

"Well," Dino said, "this is all living room. Let's turn it over *very* carefully. I don't want my people to be greeted with a mess when they show up." He went to a desk on one side of the room, switched on the computer that sat on it, and while it booted up, began opening drawers.

Ed just walked around the room slowly, looking at things, while Stone walked to the rear windows and looked out to the rear of the house. It was well lit by a bright moon. "There's a fire escape," Stone said, "going up to the top floor and leading down to a nicely planted garden. Shall I go out there and look around?"

"Let's finish in here, first," Dino said. "And we'll have a look at the top floor, then we'll go outside."

Stone was looking out one of the two windows; he withdrew and walked to the other window, where a table with a lamp sat. He pulled the table out of the way and was about to walk around it to the window, when the glass exploded inward and noise filled the room. "Shotgun!" he yelled. "Hit the deck!"

Everybody did before the second shot was fired, then there was the noise of feet ringing on the steel fire escape, then nothing. A moment later, what sounded like a garden gate slammed.

Dino sat up and reached for his handheld radio. "Shots fired!" He said into it, "Nobody's down. Assailant went down a rear fire escape and left through a garden gate. Flood a three-block area with uniforms, and proceed with caution. He has a shotgun, at the very least." He got to his feet. "Everybody okay?"

"I'm fine," Stone said.

"I'm not," Eagle replied. He was sitting up and holding his left shoulder with his right hand. "I caught a couple of pellets, I think."

Stone and Dino helped him to his feet, sat him down in a chair, and pulled his jacket off his shoulders.

"You caught three pellets," Stone said, taking a handkerchief from his pocket, rolling it, making a tourniquet and applying it to Eagle's arm. "Hold that," he said. "And once in a while, let it bleed a little. We'll get you to Lenox Hill Hospital and get you patched up."

There were many feet on the stairs now, and policemen flooded into the room.

"Stone," Dino said, "you take the car and drive up to Lenox Hill. I'll stay here and go through the place with my people."

"Right," Stone said, taking Eagle's good arm as they walked out.

"No need to steer me," Eagle said. "I'm okay." Then he collapsed onto his knees.

"Just a little shock," Stone said. "Let's try again."

44

Stone stood at the foot of an examination table in the Lenox Hill ER and watched as the resident on duty cut away Ed Eagle's shirtsleeve at the shoulder seam.

"Fucking Turnbull & Asser shirt," Ed grumbled.

"Send it back to them, and they'll make a new sleeve for you," Stone said.

Eagle winced as the doctor probed.

"Not too bad," the young man said.

"For you," Ed replied sulkily.

Stone thought the doctor looked like a college freshman, but his ID read "MD."

"Let's get some lidocaine in there," the doctor said to the nurse on duty.

"What dosage?" she asked.

"Whatever you think best," he replied. "There are three wounds."

She handed him a syringe, half full, and he injected each wound twice. "It'll stop hurting in a minute," he said.

"I'm glad to hear that," Eagle replied.

The doctor used a probe to examine each wound. "Not in very deep," he said. "Your coat and shirtsleeve probably absorbed some of the velocity."

"Shit, I forgot about my coat sleeve," Eagle said.

"I know a good reweaver," Stone said. "The repair will be invisible."

"It's stopped hurting," Eagle said, heaving a deep sigh.

"Good," the doctor said. He selected a tool from a tray and went to work. Shortly, the *clink* of pellet on metal tray was heard three times. "There we go. Now I'll clean and suture, and you'll live to fight another day."

"Great," Eagle said.

The resident went to work, cleansing and closing the wounds and suturing them, then the nurse stepped in, cleaning the area and applying a bandage. "We'll give you some extra bandages, so you can apply a fresh one every day."

Eagle took Stone's outstretched hand with his own good one and pulled himself into a sitting position.

"Do you want a sling?" the nurse asked.

For a second, Eagle smiled. "Oh, I thought you said 'fling.' I think it will be okay as is."

"Not when the lidocaine wears off," she said, tucking a sling into the bag with the bandages. "There's a prescription for a painkiller, too."

"You have a point," Eagle said.

Stone helped Ed's right arm into his jacket, but left the other arm unsleeved and a bit bloody.

They made Ed get into a wheelchair.

"I'll push him," Stone said. He took hold of the chair and rolled it down the hall to the outside doors. Dino's car awaited them, and Dino was inside.

"How you doing, Ed?" he asked.

"Just great," Eagle said, "until the lidocaine wears off."

"Let's stop at a drugstore and fill his prescription," Stone said. "I don't want to listen to more pissing and moaning."

Back at Stone's house they returned to the study, where Susannah awaited. She inspected Eagle: "What's this?"

"Three shotgun pellets removed. I was lucky." He was looking for sympathy, and he had found it.

They took up were they had left off with brandy. Eagle washed down one of his painkillers.

"What did you find in the apartment?"

Stone asked Dino.

"His two minions were occupying the guest room, each in his bed, each with two bullets to the back of each head. They could have been staying there all along. My other theory is that Larkin had left something there that was incriminating, or just something he needed, like money. If that's so, he took it with him. I expect he had a car parked on Sixty-fifth Street, so he's in the wind."

"I'll bet he got a ticket in that block," Stone said.

"Good point. I'll have it checked." He got on his phone, asked some questions, then hung up. "Nine tickets were issued in that block during the relevant time frame, none of them registered to Larkin or Frances, but two of them are rentals. We're checking those out."

"It might be a starting place."

"Stone," Dino said. "I was thinking I might announce your death at the scene. It might give you some breathing room."

"No," Stone said emphatically. "He'll just go on to the next name on the hit list, and I don't want that on my conscience. Anyway, I'd like him to try again. Next time, I might get a shot at him."

"Then he will be free from harm," Dino

said to the others. "Stone is a lousy shot."

"I don't get your range time," Stone said defensively.

"He's got a nice little range downstairs in his basement, and there's no waiting. He's just lazy."

"I'll cop to lazy," Stone said.

"I guess that's better than just being a lousy shot."

Susannah spoke up. "I think my fella needs some sleep," she said, "or he'll fall off his chair." She got Eagle to his feet and walked him to the elevator.

"I'll change his bandage tomorrow," Jenna said.

"I'd better get home," Dino said, rising. "Viv is due in from Berlin." He left the house.

"That leaves just us," Jenna said to Stone. "Whatever will we do with ourselves?"

45

Stone and Jenna were busy at work the following morning when Stone's cell rang. He kept right on going. Jenna stopped. "I can't do it when the phone's ringing," she said.

"It's just a phone," Stone said, trying lamely to rekindle her interest.

"I'm sorry. Sometimes I'm on call at night, and once awoken I never get back to sleep."

"It's not the middle of the night, and you don't have to go back to sleep," Stone said, making a valiant final effort. It failed, and he picked up his phone. "What?"

"It's Dino."

"I should have known."

"Is that all you two do, even in the daylight hours?"

"Just barely the daylight hours."

"Well, before you turn on the morning news, there's news."

"I hope it's good."

281

"It's bad and it's good."

"Who did he kill this time?"

"Nobody on the list. That's the good news and the bad news, because he killed two other people — collateral damage."

"No connection?"

"None."

"Then why?"

"An apparent case of road rage. Our guy was headed north on the West Side Highway, about Seventy-ninth Street, when he slammed on his brakes, maybe to avoid an animal. The remains of some kind of rodent were found."

"So he killed the rodent. Who else?"

"Nah, when he slammed on the brakes, he got rear-ended. According to witnesses in the opposite lane, who were stopped because of a traffic accident, he reached into the glove compartment for something, presumably a weapon, walked calmly to the car who hit him, and shot two people, man and woman, through their windshield, both DOA."

"God, that's terrible. We've got to get this guy off the street, one way or another."

"I'm leaning heavily toward the other," Dino said.

"You shouldn't say that on the phone."

"I didn't say it, I must have been thinking it."

"Then the route between your brain and your tongue has recently been cleared."

"Entirely possible, but you can't quote another man's thoughts, especially on a witness stand."

"You have a point," Stone confessed. "Do you have an idea?"

"Yes. It's much the same as my last idea, and as with my last idea, we have to find him before we can murder him."

"You didn't say that."

"There I go thinking again. Please ignore my brain."

"Well, if I thought it would help, I'd drive around the city rear-ending people until he took a shot at me, but it seems a little haphazard."

"Not so much as you'd think. There's a lot of road rage out there. These days, you could probably get yourself shot inside of half an hour, even if by the wrong shooter."

"I think I had in mind something both more productive and more specific, in terms of the shooter."

"I can see how you might feel that way. I'll keep you posted." Dino hung up.

"Dino?" Jenna said.

"Dino. Larkin shot two more innocent

people last night."

"Don't look so dejected, Stone."

"Why not? I got two citizens shot to death on the West Side Highway."

"It's not your fault."

"Why not? When disasters surrounding me get people killed, it's usually my fault."

"That doesn't make any sense, and please don't try to make it better. You'll just depress us both even more."

Stone shrugged, because he couldn't think of anything to say.

Jenna threw off the covers. "I'm going to take a shower and go to work."

"Breakfast?"

"I'll grab a bite somewhere."

Stone rang for his usual. When Jenna came out of the bathroom, all clean and perky, she grabbed half of his English muffin, heaped some scrambled egg onto it, and was eating it when she walked out with an airy wave.

"That was half my breakfast!" Stone called after her.

"Reorder!" she called back and closed the door behind her a little too firmly.

When Stone got downstairs, there was a wrapped hot roll from a nearby deli on his desk, and he had it with his second cup of coffee. It was delicious. Then he saw the note in the bag.

Just got a call from my office, and they insist they can't get along without me any longer. I've asked Joan to book me on a flight home; ask her to send my bag, will you? It was great fun; let's do it again! And again, and again!

Her address and phone number were on the note, and he asked Joan to deal with the reservation and the bag.

46

Stone had just finished his roll when Joan buzzed him. "A Mr. Gunderson from the First Plains Bank and Trust Company of Ames, Iowa."

"Didn't you tell him he had a wrong number?"

"No, he knew exactly who he wanted to talk to, and that is you."

Stone picked up the phone. "Mr. Gunderson, what can I do for you?" he asked quickly, as if he had been on another line.

"Well, Mr. Barrington," he said, "you can tell me where all this money came from."

"What money is that, Mr. Gunderson?"

"The money that was mentioned in her will, some 847, 500 dollars of it. I know it didn't belong to Frances, because I loaned her ten thousand dollars a coupla weeks ago, jah? So's she could eat something and pay her rent."

"Jah, if you say so, Mr. Gunderson." Stone

286

was beginning to feel that he had stepped into a scene from the movie *Fargo.*

"I recall that a sum of money was mentioned in her will, but I don't recall a number."

"Well, we been readin' about this feller, Larkin, who she got herself tangled up with, and our bank don't take no funds from dubious sources."

"Mr. Gunderson, a last will and testament is not a dubious source, and it was properly signed, sworn, and attested to by the appropriate number of witnesses, as is often done in hospitals in these parts." He clamped his hand over his mouth to prevent further Midwestern colloquialisms from escaping.

"It's the *source* of the funds we're talkin' about here," Gunderson said. "This Sig Larkin sounds dubious to me."

"Be that as it may," Stone said, "it sounds like a number to me, and that's what banks deal in, as I recall. Now, my suggestion would be to accept the funds into her account and to wait for a while in case somebody asks for some or all of it back. At that time, you can assess the validity of the claim and pay, or not pay, accordingly."

"How long is 'for a while'?" Gunderson asked.

"You get to decide that."

"Reason I ask is, somebody has already requested some — strike that — all of it."

"Oh? And who might that be?"

"It would be a New York lawyer," Gunderson said, "and I expect you can imagine what folks in these parts might think of that."

"Well, Mr. Gunderson, you're talkin' to a New York lawyer right now, and we don't take kindly to insults from west of the Mississippi. Nor east of that river, neither. Now, why did you call me, instead of him?" God help me, Stone thought, I'm locked into this lingo!

"Frances mentioned you in a note. Well, I hardly know what to do next," Gunderson confessed.

Then the penny dropped. "Why don't you begin by telling me the lawyer's name and phone number, and I'll see what I can find out."

"Would that service be gratis?" Gunderson asked.

"Up to a point which we have not yet reached."

"All right, the firm name is Woodman & Weld." Gunderson kindly spelled it for him, which he didn't need, since he was a member of that firm. "And the name is Herbert

Fisher, Esq., which I take to mean *Esquire.* I thought that reference was for gentlemen, not New York lawyers." He gave Stone his own office number.

"It takes all kinds to make a firm of New York lawyers, Mr. Gunderson," Stone said. "Now, if you will give me an hour or so, I'll see what I can learn about this transaction."

"Jah, I can do that, I guess. But after an hour, my mind is going to start taking a suspicious view of things again. I'll speak to you in an hour."

"Or so," Stone said. "Mr. Fisher could be occupied with a client."

"That's what I thought."

"I don't control the actions or meeting times of other attorneys, Mr. Gunderson. It'll be 'or so,' and it's still gratis."

"Jah," Gunderson said, emphatically. "I'll count on that."

"Start counting, Mr. Gunderson," Stone said, then hung up. He buzzed Joan. "Get me Herbie," he said, "and kindly produce him on the line in less than an hour and a quarter."

"Oookay," Joan said slowly. "Is it okay if it's faster than that?"

"Jah," Stone said, and hung up.

An hour and four minutes had passed

before Joan buzzed him and handed him Herbie on the line.

"How are you, Stone?" Herbert Fisher was a protégé of Stone's, in a manner of speaking, who had formerly been a sly shyster of an attorney with a dubious claim to membership in the bar. Under Stone's tutelage, he had transformed himself into a graduate of New York University Law School, passed the bar, and gone to work for Woodman & Weld, where he was recently elected partner.

"Herb," Stone said, since the young man had developed an aversion to *Herbie*. "What do you know about the last will and testament of one Frances — Oh, I forget her last name."

"I believe I know of whom you speak," Herbie said. "New York Hospital sent me her file, which contained a proper will."

"Do you know what the estate was worth?"

"No, I haven't got around to that."

"Well, it turns out to be something north of eight hundred thousand dollars," Stone said.

"Oh, good, then we'll get paid."

"That's exactly what a Mr. Gunderson of the First Plains Bank & Trust Company would have said you'd say."

"I don't believe I've had the pleasure," Herbie replied.

"Well, you're about to," Stone said. "When he calls, he'll explain himself in slightly accented English, or perhaps, Swedish: one of those. Careful, it's catching."

"Okay."

"Something else, Herb."

"What?"

"It's very likely that you'll get a call soon, from someone who will represent himself as being the rightful heir to Frances's fortune."

"Oh, yeah," Herbie said. "He just called."

"Well, I believe you just spoke to Sig Larkin, the hit man in the hit-list controversy. Did you get his particulars?"

"He said he was away from his computer, so I e-mailed him a form at a computer shop in midtown which will take him an hour or so to fill out, and I told him we'd go on from there."

"You done good, Herbie," Stone said. "I'll call you back. Oh, and don't send him any money. Stall."

"I'm good at that. I'm a New York lawyer."

Stone hung up and called Gunderson.

"Jah, this is Nihls Gunderson."

"And this is Stone Barrington, back to you in slightly more than an hour or so."

"Jah, good."

"I've spoken to Mr. Fisher on your behalf, and he is ready to take your call. Please leave the matter entirely in his hands, and don't call back the other man who called you about the money."

"How did *you* know about that call, Mr. Barrington?"

"We New York lawyers have a secret means of communication called the telephone," Stone replied. "Oh, I should tell you that his firm, Woodman & Weld, is highly thought of on this side of the Continental Divide, and so is Mr. Herbert Fisher. Kindly treat him accordingly."

"Jah, I'll do that. I looked her up, and I see that you're one of her senior partners, so I guess I started in the right place."

"I guess you did, Mr. Gunderson. Look up before you leap, is always a good policy."

"Jah, I expect so."

"And if, by any chance, someone turns up at your office, inquiring about Frances's funds, leave the room to check on something, and call the police. That man will be a cold-blooded killer, and you should have no truck with him."

"I tink that's good advice," Gunderson said.

"Auf wiedersehen." Stone hung up. He hoped the man wasn't Swedish.

47

Stone called Dino, reflecting that, at times like these, it was good to be able to go straight to the top, instead of dealing with a 911 operator.

"Bacchetti."

"Dino, I have big news."

"I could use some big news, if it's of a positive nature."

"Larkin has discovered that Frances stole all his money."

"All his money?"

"Jah. Well, at least enough of it to make him want to recover it."

" 'Jah'?"

"Sorry about that. The bank is in Iowa, and they talk that way out there."

"If you say so."

"Take my word for it. Larkin called the bank a few minutes ago and laid claim to the funds. A banker named Gunderson directed him to a New York law firm apparently hired by Frances to handle her estate."

"Which law firm?"

"One by the name of Woodman & Weld, care of one Herbert Fisher, Esq."

"Sounds like you're chasing your tail," Dino said.

"I'm acutely aware of that. Herbie is now clued in. He's already had a call from Larkin and e-mailed him a lengthy form to fill out to prove his identity."

"E-mailed where?"

"To an unnamed computer shop in New York."

"And how do we know he's in New York and not Iowa, or wherever they talk like that."

"We don't."

"And we can't cover the shop, because there must be fifty of them in midtown, even more downtown and in the boroughs."

"Dino, I can only tell you what I can tell you, jah?"

"Are you at a fascist rally?"

"That was a 'yes' in your native tongue."

"My native tongue is Sicilian."

"Jah. All we can do now is wait for Herbie to hear from Larkin and arrange a meet."

"Have him tell Larkin to come to his office."

"Are you nuts? I don't want a crazed gunman wandering around the Seagram Building, looking for the right office number and being pissed off when he can't find it."

"All right, tell Herbie to ask him to lunch. It's getting to be about that time."

"Where?"

"At the Grill, in the Seagram Building."

"Same problem, Dino, just a different floor."

"Well, he can't invite him to some noodle shop. He might catch on."

"Jah," Stone said before he could catch himself. "We have now reached the point where *you* have to get an idea. I'm fresh out."

Dino pondered that for long seconds. "I don't suppose One Police Plaza would work, either."

"Good guess."

"Well, now that we're guessing, I guess we can't solve this problem, at least not by conventional means. If we flood midtown with every available car, Larkin just might notice."

"That's a good bet."

"Okay, let Herbie tell Larkin to choose the spot. He knows where he is."

"Indubitably."

"Herbie can say he's going out to lunch

somewhere, and Larkin can meet him out-side."

"Outside anywhere in midtown is still a target-rich environment, unless you know of an empty restaurant."

"I got it!" Dino said.

"What?"

"An empty restaurant. That place we went to that time is being painted. It'll be de-serted at lunch hour, because all the paint-ers will have gone somewhere that's open."

"Are you talking about P. J. Clarke's?"

"No, that other one, farther west."

"The Yard of Ale?"

"That's the one. I tried to go in, and there were painters everywhere."

"Well, I suggest you fill the place with cops in painters' overalls."

"How much time we got?"

"Strike that last remark about painters. Fill it with cops in business suits, male and female. It's located in an office building. Leave a table or two empty, one for Her-bie."

"Got it."

"And we don't want any black shoes with white socks, got that? They might as well wear badges."

"Got it."

"I'll call you right back." Stone hung up

and called Herbie.

"Herb Fisher."

"Herb, do you know a restaurant called the Yard of Ale?"

"Yeah."

"Tell Larkin to meet you there."

"I can't do that."

"Why not?"

"Because it's closed for painting."

"Don't worry, if you can buy us an hour, it will be filled with cops, not painters. All you have to do is let the guy sit down, then duck and run."

"An hour?"

"Until lunch hour. That'll give Dino time to work his magic."

"Okay, I'll tell him twelve-thirty."

"Even better." Stone hung up and called Dino. "Herbie says twelve-thirty."

"Great. Can I buy you lunch?"

"Where?"

"At the Yard of Ale, noon."

"Is the food decent?"

"I recommend the ale."

"There's a side entrance from inside the office building."

"Then we'll meet there. Come armed."

"Don't worry."

"Stone?"

"Jah?"

"First of all, stop it with the 'jah' business."

"Okay."

"Second, if you had taken my advice when Ed Eagle got shot, Larkin would think you were dead, and you wouldn't be putting yourself in jeopardy like this."

"Oh, swell, rub it in!" Stone hung up.

Herbie was at his desk when the phone rang. "Herb Fisher."

"Mr. Fisher, this is Egil Krogar."

Herbie blanked.

"About Frances Bowers's will?"

"Oh, sorry, Mr. Krogar. I was thinking about someone else."

"Someone named Krogar? As far as I know, I'm the only person in the United States with that name."

"No, someone called Emil."

"That's not my name."

"I know."

"I've completed your form. Where should I send it?"

Herbie looked at his watch: a quarter to twelve.

"Mr. Krogar, I'm just on my way to an out-of-office meeting. Could we meet at, say, twelve-thirty? I'll buy you lunch."

"Well, I guess so. That's very generous of you."

"We'll both be hungry by then, and we'll need a few minutes to run through the form together."

"Where shall we meet?" Krogar asked.

"There's a place called the Yard of Ale, on East Fifty-third Street."

"That won't work," Krogar said.

"You don't like sausage and ale?"

"It's not that. I tried to go there yesterday, and it's being painted."

Herbie thought fast. "First day open," he said. "I just made a reservation. They promise it doesn't smell like paint, just sausage and ale. And it's in the building where my appointment is."

"All right, I'll see you at twelve-thirty."

"I'll be at a table at the rear of the restaurant, where it's quieter."

"Fine." Krogar hung up.

Herbie called Stone.

"Yes, Herb?"

"He's on for twelve-thirty. He says his name is Egil Krogar." He spelled the name. "I'll see you there."

"Don't you come anywhere near the place," Stone said.

"I told him I had a meeting in the building. He'll be watching for me."

"All right, go into the building, and take the elevator upstairs."

"Where upstairs?"

"Anywhere upstairs. Just get out of the lobby."

"I'll have to show myself at twelve-thirty, or he won't show himself."

"Jesus, Herb, how do you get yourself into these things?"

"By following your instructions. I'll see you at noon in the lobby entrance. You can figure out what to do with me then."

"Okay, jah."

"What?"

"That's Norwegian for twelve o'clock." Stone hung up.

48

Stone phoned for Fred and got into the car. "Yard of Ale, on East Fifty-third Street," he said.

"I'm afraid it's closed — being painted," Fred replied. "How about P. J. Clarke's?"

"Fred, I have inside information. The Yard of Ale is no longer being painted, and I have a reservation."

"If you say so, sir."

"Fred, drive."

Fred drove and made it in no time. "Lose yourself nearby, until I call," Stone said, then got out of the car. He was greeted by a large sign that read: CLOSED FOR REPAINTING. "Oh, shit," Stone said, checking his watch: eleven fifty-five. He ran into the building through the office entrance. Dino was standing next to the door to the restaurant, and he had a man in a suit backed up against the wall next to the door. Dino had turned a bright red color.

301

"I can't," the manager was saying.

"You want to be fired?" Dino yelled. "I can speak to the owner."

"I'm the owner."

"All right," Dino said, making a visible effort to control himself. "We . . ."

"May I speak, please?" Stone asked, flashing his badge.

"Yes, please," the man said. "Who is this person?"

"This person is Dino Bacchetti, the police commissioner for the City of New York."

"You mean he wasn't lying about that?"

"He just looks like he's lying. Has he explained the situation?"

"Sort of. He wants the painters out and the restaurant up and running."

"No, he just wants it to look like it's running for a few minutes, until we can capture the most wanted man in the city."

"Just get the painters out," Dino said through clenched teeth.

"I can't do that," the man said. "If you want the place to look like it's running. The painters are the waiters."

"Please make them look like waiters," Stone said, "as quickly as possible, and ask them to set the tables for lunch, pronto. The tables will then be filled with police officers."

"All right," the man said. He stepped into the restaurant and shouted some words at the painters, who stared at him blankly, until he shouted them again. Then there was a bustle of activity as they went to work.

"You see," Stone said to Dino. "You just have to be nice."

"I *was* nice. The guy seemed to think I was some maniac."

"We'll give him a pass on that one," Stone said.

"What kind of language does he speak?"

"I don't know," Stone replied. "Greek, Romanian, maybe."

"Is Romanian a language?"

"Dino," Stone said patiently, "start giving your people orders. Let's make this happen."

Herbie Fisher suddenly appeared at Stone's elbow. "Where do you want me?"

"Out of here," Stone said.

"Apart from that?"

"Over there at that table, with an ale in your hand," Stone said. "When the guy arrives and you've identified him, pull on your right earlobe, like this." Stone pulled on his earlobe.

"That's your left earlobe," Herbie pointed out.

"Sorry, like this," Stone said, pulling his

right. "If you're not sure it's the guy, pull the other one."

"The left?"

"That's right."

"You're confusing me."

"If you're not sure it's the guy pull your left earlobe." He demonstrated, correctly.

"Am I going to get paint on my suit?" Herbie asked. "It's brand-new."

"The New York City Police Department will reimburse you for any damages," Stone said.

"Now, wait a minute . . ." Dino started to say.

"You shut up and get your cops at those tables, fast. And watch out for white socks."

A bus outside unloaded, and groups of people, men and women, came inside and were directed to tables by Dino. Three of the men had to be asked to change socks.

"Looking pretty good," Stone said.

"There's no food," Dino remarked.

Stone crooked a finger at the owner. "Give them menus and bread rolls, quick."

"We didn't order bread for today. We're supposed to be closed for painting."

"You have any boxes of breadsticks?"

"Maybe, but they'll be stale."

"Distribute them, please. I want them munching."

"I'll get some bread from the Greek place next door." He disappeared.

"Why didn't we just use the Greek place?" Dino asked.

"Because you didn't think of it," Stone replied. "It was your turn to think."

As the clock wound down to 12:30, the place began to look like a restaurant again. Ladders and pails had disappeared, and the customers seemed to be enjoying themselves.

Herbie, across the room from where Stone and Dino waited by the door, tried a breadstick and spat it out.

"The roll, dummkopf," Stone breathed. Herbie liked the roll better.

Twelve-thirty came and went. No Larkin. At twelve-thirty-nine, a man in a dark suit came through the front door, looked around and saw Herbie with his finger up, beckoning. He walked to the rear of the room.

"Mr. Krogar?" Herbie asked.

"That's me," the man said. Without sitting down he reached into an inside pocket and came out with several sheets of folded paper. "Look this over while I use the men's room," he said, starting toward the rear of the restaurant.

"Excuse me," Herbie said. "The name on these papers is not Krogar, it's Larkin,

305

Sigmund Larkin. Who am I talking to here?" He pulled on his left earlobe.

"I'm Egil Krogar, the lawyer," the man said.

"I'm going to need to see your client," Herbie said. "I'm not handing over all this money to anybody but him."

"Look it over," Krogar said. "He'll be here in a minute, so if you don't mind, I'm going to relieve myself."

Herbie glanced at Stone and shook his head, pulled his left earlobe again, then he started to read.

"What the fuck is going on?" Dino asked.

"I don't know. Herbie pulled his left earlobe, which means hold off."

"That guy, Krogar, matches the description, sort of."

"He seems skinnier to me," Stone said. "Wiry, even."

"So maybe he's lost some weight."

Herbie sat quietly, reading the papers. He turned a page.

Krogar returned and sat down. "Smells like paint in there," he said.

"Okay," Herbie said, "all this is neatly printed and legible. Where's your client?"

"In the car. I told you he'd be here in a

minute. Why don't we order?"

A waiter stepped up to the table, as if summoned.

"I'll have the choucroute garni," Herbie said. "I recommend it."

"Make that two," Krogar said.

"What about Mr. Larkin?" Herbie asked.

"I'm Larkin," the man replied.

"Okay, prove it," Herbie said.

The man placed a United States passport on the table, open to the picture page.

"Right," Herbie said, then pulled his right earlobe, and all hell broke loose.

49

Somebody blew a whistle, and thirty cops were on their feet, pistols pointed. The man who said he was Larkin had a pistol pointed, too: hard under Herbie Fisher's chin.

Larkin grabbed Herbie by the collar with his free hand. "Bring the papers," he said.

Herbie grabbed the papers and allowed himself to be dragged to the rear of the restaurant. "Guns on the floor!" Larkin yelled, and thirty cops dropped their guns, more or less as one man, even the women. "Nobody move!" Larkin yelled, and nobody did. He dragged Herbie through the kitchen and out the back door, then there was a noise of something being propped against it.

Stone and Dino ran toward the rear door and put their shoulders against it, bruising their shoulders. From outside, there was the sound of a good-sized motorcycle cranking up.

"Give me the papers, and run that way," Larkin shouted at Herbie, indicating down the alley with his chin. Herbie handed over the papers and ran, while Larking tucked them into his pocket and got the machine into gear. He blew past Herbie, who was trying to become part of a brick wall, and headed out onto Park Avenue.

"Shit," Dino said, rubbing his shoulder. "I thought we were ready for him."

"He was readier than we were," Stone explained. "Get on the radio."

Dino picked up his handheld and barked orders to stop a motorcycle in flight.

"What kind of motorcycle?" somebody asked.

"Stone?"

"Medium-sized," Stone said. "No other description." He called for Fred on his cell phone.

Half an hour later, Stone, Dino, and Herbie were having lunch at P. J. Clarke's.

"We're exactly where we were an hour ago," Dino said, "and Larkin is in the wind again."

"He's probably stolen another motorcycle or car by now," Stone replied.

"He could be in New Jersey," Dino said.

"Did you alert New Jersey?"

"I alerted the world," Dino said.

"Why did he want the papers?" Herbie asked.

"Because he wants the eight hundred grand and change," Dino offered.

"From who?" Herbie asked. "*I'm* sure as hell not going to give it to him."

"Gunderson, the banker," Stone said. "In Ames, Iowa." He dug out his phone and found a recent call from the banker.

"Jah, this is Gunderson," the man said.

"Mr. Gunderson, this is Stone Barrington in New York."

"Jah? And what can I do for you?"

"Hang on to Frances's money," Stone said.

"Too late," Gunderson said. "The feller faxed me the paperwork, and I sent it to him."

"You mean you wired him the funds?"

"Jah."

"To what bank?"

"Some investment corporation in Delaware." He read off the name and account number. "That do you, then?"

"That'll do me. Oh, and there's no charge."

"I didn't think there would be," Gunderson replied. "You said gratis."

"That's right, I did." Stone hung up. "The money went to a Delaware investment firm," he said.

"Then call the bank and put a stop on it," Dino said.

"That won't happen."

"So now Larkin is in the wind with eight hundred grand."

"And change," Stone replied.

"And what are our chances of laying hands on Larkin?" Dino asked.

"Slim and slimmer," Stone said. "If he's already left the country. I expect he's moved the funds to an offshore bank somewhere in the world."

"I'm going to need better geography than that," Dino said.

"It took both of you to fuck this up this good," Herbie observed.

"You're the one who let him get away," Stone pointed out.

"I make it a point to let armed men get away," Herbie said.

"The point is, if I'm that guy and I have eight hundred grand, where would I go?"

"I'm waiting for the answer," Stone said.

"The answer is, anywhere I like," Herbie replied.

"Not by public transport," Dino said. "He needs a private plane, a charter."

"He can afford one," Herbie said.

"So can Stone," Dino said.

"I think our best guess is Georgetown, in the Cayman Islands. Loose banks, reachable from New York without refueling, in the right airplane."

"I say, let's go there," Dino said.

"It may be our best guess," Stone replied, "but it's still one hell of a long shot."

"Have you got anything better to do?" Dino asked.

"Not really."

"Can I go, too?" Herbie asked. "I cleared my afternoon."

"Why not," Stone said. "Let's take Dino's car to Teterboro. It has a siren."

Once aboard, Stone got out his cell phone and began issuing orders to pilots and refuelers. It took them forty minutes to reach Teterboro, and when they did the G-500 had an engine running. They boarded, and the other engine started up.

Herbie took a seat and had a look around. "How much?" he asked.

"Don't ask," Stone replied. "You'd have to win the lottery all over again." Herbie had already won it once.

Dino sat down with him and buckled his seat belt. "Okay," he said, "what does this guy look like?"

"You saw him," Stone said.

"His back was to me. I saw a fedora, some eyeglasses, and a kind of hawk nose."

"You can't keep a fedora on while fleeing on a motorcycle," Stone said, "and he looked skinnier to me than last time."

"It's all that running," Dino said.

Four hours later, they set down at Georgetown.

50

They had a rental car waiting in Georgetown, and the three of them piled in.

"Maybe we should have three rentals,"
Dino said.

"Herb is the only one who's had a clear
look at the guy from close up," Stone said.
"One car is best. Start looking, Herb."

They were heading down a sort of main
drag, and Herbie's head was swiveling.
"Every other building here is a bank," he
said.

"Look for a guy in a business suit and a
hat," Stone said.

"I thought the hat would have blown
away," Dino chipped in, "on the motorcycle."

"I know it's hard to believe," Stone said,
"but he might still have the hat."

"Herb," Dino said. "Did the glasses look
to you like a disguise, or something he
needed to see?"

"No idea," Herbie said, "but there's a guy in a suit, no hat."

"Herb," Stone said. "He's black, and it doesn't look like a disguise."

"There is that," Herbie said, and went back to swiveling.

They reached the end of the street, made a U-turn, and started back the other way. Herbie nodded toward the sidewalk. "That looks kind of like him," he said, pointing at a man walking into a bank, "except for the Hawaiian shirt."

"Let's get in there," Stone said, pulling into a handicapped parking space.

"You can't park here," Dino said.

"Stop sounding like a cop. You see any other parking spaces?"

"Not really."

They got out of the car and crossed the street. "Don't go peering through the window," Dino said. "He'll spot us from inside."

"I'll go in," Herbie said, handing Stone his suit jacket and tie. He walked into the bank and came out ten seconds later.

"The guy in the Hawaiian shirt is sitting at a desk, talking to somebody who looks like a banker, but his back is to me. "He's wearing a straw hat."

Stone handed Herbie back his clothing and peered through the window. "Could be

315

him," he said.

"So, what are we going to do about it?" Herbie asked. "Dino, do you have any authority here?"

"Nothing but a badge and my native sense of command," Dino replied.

"That'll have to do," Stone said. "What's our plan?"

"Let's let him see us," Dino said, "and see how he reacts. If he runs, he's our guy. Probably."

Dino motioned for them to spread out a little when they entered the bank. As they did, the man stood up and shook the banker's hand. He was holding a briefcase, something Stone hadn't noticed before.

"Hi, Sig," Stone said.

The man didn't turn, but froze instead. He said something to the banker, and the man indicated the rear of the bank.

"Restroom," Stone said.

"Back door," Dino replied. They watched as the man went into the restroom, then they crowded into the hallway behind him. Dino tried the door. "Locked," he whispered. "We'll have to wait him out or kick in the door. What's your preference?"

"My preference is not being arrested for kicking in the door," Stone replied. "Be patient."

Dino took a step back and kicked in the door. It flew back, banged into the wall. Dino stepped in with his gun in his hand. "Freeze!" he yelled.

"Window," Stone said. It stood open, flapping a little in the breeze. "Nice window, big."

Dino hopped up onto the toilet and looked both ways out the window. "Alley," he said. "I don't see him. We'll have to split up."

They ran to the rear door and opened it. "Stone, you and Herb go right. I'll go left, and we'll meet back at the car." He turned left and started to run.

Stone and Herbie ran, dodging a garbage truck coming from the other way.

Herbie stopped and yelled, "Stone!"

Stone looked back at him. "What's wrong?"

"He's driving the garbage truck!" Herbie yelled, watching as the truck made a turn at the end of the block.

Stone, panting in the heat, got out his phone and called Dino. He took three rings to answer. "What?"

"Sig is driving the garbage truck!" Stone yelled into the phone.

"What garbage truck?" Dino yelled back.

"The one that's about to run over you!" He wasn't sure about that, because he couldn't see it, but he thought it was the safe thing to say.

A torrent of bad language issued from the phone. "Dammit!" Dino yelled. "He nearly got me, and I can't get a shot at him from behind." He fired a shot anyway.

"Let's keep going this way," Stone said to Herbie, and they ran. They made it to the main street in concert with Dino, who was coming from the other direction, and they all piled into their car.

"Back the way we came," Dino said. "Toward the airport!"

They made the airport, which was secured by a chain-link fence. The garbage truck was inside, parked on the ramp, and a twin-engine Piper, a Navaho painted yellow, was starting up. "He's in the Navaho," Stone shouted, "but the gate's locked." They drove around to the FBO, abandoned the car and ran for the G-500. Faith, Stone's pilot, was standing by the airplane and saw them coming. She yelled something inside the airplane, and an engine could be heard to start turning. She waved the three of them aboard, locked the door behind them, and dove into the cockpit.

"Let's go!" Stone yelled. "Follow the Navaho!"

"We can't move without a clearance," she said, donning her headset.

"The Navaho didn't seem to have one."

"Or he did it all in advance," she replied, pressing the push-to-talk switch and requesting taxi and takeoff clearances. "Five-minute delay," she said to Stone, who was hovering over her.

"Go anyway," he replied.

"We'll just get arrested, and they'll get away. Open the door and see if you can tell which way the Navaho is going."

Stone ran back, opened the door, and stood there scanning the skies.

Dino joined him. "Is that it?" he asked, pointing aloft.

"Is it yellow?" Stone asked. "I think the Navaho was yellow."

Dino ducked back inside and came back with a pair of binoculars. "It's yellow," he said. "Which way is it headed?"

Stone looked around to orient himself. "North," he said. He shut and locked the door and went back to the cockpit. "Request a departure to the north," he said to Faith. "It looks like it's headed for the Bahamas."

Faith did so, then she released the brakes and started to taxi. "We're cleared for takeoff," she said.

"We're a lot faster than the Navaho,"

Stone said. "Try to avoid running past it."

"It could turn for Florida," she said.

"I want to see it do that before we head that way," Stone said.

Faith shoved the throttles forward and started her takeoff roll.

51

They were halfway to the Bahamas before Faith's copilot spotted the yellow Navaho. "Ten o'clock and maybe twelve thousand feet," she said.

Faith retarded the throttles, and tried to keep the smaller airplane in sight. The Bahamas loomed ahead. She got on the radio and requested twelve thousand feet, then turned toward Stone, who was occupying the jump seat behind her. "We don't have a clearance to land," she said, "because of the hurricane."

Stone had forgotten about the recent hurricane. He ran back to where Dino was sitting. "Get on the satphone to the head of your aviation department and tell him to call somebody at the FAA and get us permission to land, which is being denied, because of the recent hurricane. Tell them it's a pursuit of a dangerous fugitive."

Dino grabbed a phone and went to work.

Stone went forward to the jump seat. "Are we still with him?"

"Yes, and he won't be able to see us. No rearview mirrors in airplanes."

"Dino's working on a clearance."

"There are three airports," Faith said, "and I think they are all up and running by now. Look, the Navaho is descending." Then she answered a radio call. "Wow!" she said. "We've got clearance to land any-where."

"Land where the Navaho lands."

She began to descend again. "Looks like he's headed for Marsh Harbour," she said.

"Drop back some more, so we can land behind him. We could lose him, if we have to go around."

Faith followed his instructions. "All right," she said, "this is as slow as I'm going to go; any slower, and we risk a low-altitude stall." She swung left. "I'm going to give him more space," she said, then after a couple of minutes she turned right again. "The instrument approach isn't working yet, but I can use our onboard synthetic vision; that will keep us pointed at the airport, until I can see it."

"Good," Stone said. He picked up the Navaho again. "He's about twelve o'clock and four or five miles."

"Got him."

As the Navaho slowed further, the distance between the two airplanes grew shorter. "We may have to go around," Faith said.

"Just do your best."

She put down some flaps and lowered the landing gear, slowing the airplane further.

"He's over the numbers," she said, "except there aren't any numbers left after the storm."

Stone let his vision wander ahead, and he was stunned by what he saw. There didn't seem to be a building standing in the Abacos Island group.

"He's been waved off by the tower," she said, "climbing and turning left. Maybe he'll try for Nassau. That's in the best shape of the available runways." She followed, staying at three thousand feet. Shortly, Nassau Airport appeared in the distance. Stone could see a large aircraft setting down, probably a storm-relief craft.

"We've got clearance to land," Faith said. "Strap in, the runway may be bumpy."

Stone yelled at Dino and Herbie to strap in, then did so himself. Faith turned downwind, then started a turn for the runway. The yellow Navaho was turning off the runway onto a ramp, where a police car waited.

"You deal with customs and the police," Faith said to her copilot. I'm keeping my eyes open for the occupants of the Navaho." She set down and slowed as fast as possible. The runway wasn't bad, and she taxied back to the ramp.

Stone saw the Hawaiian shirt talking to the policeman on the ramp, then they gave him some papers, and he strode toward what was left of the airport buildings.

Faith came to a stop.

"Dino," Stone shouted, "pave the way for us, will you?"

Dino unbuckled and ran forward to the door. Stone had it open the moment the engines stopped. Dino walked down the stairs waving his badge, with Stone and Herbie right behind.

"Come on," Dino said. "I've borrowed us a police car and a driver."

They piled into a battered patrol car.

"Man in a Hawaiian shirt," Dino said.

"I saw him go into the building," the driver said.

"Drive around to the other side, and let's try to pick him up."

As they emerged from behind the building, Dino spotted Sig getting into a van. "He had a vehicle waiting," he said.

Stone was in the shotgun seat. "Please

don't lose him," he said to the driver, sticking a hundred into the man's shirt pocket.

The driver grinned. "Are you trying to bribe a public official?" he asked.

"I'm encouraging one," Stone replied.

"And he is encouraged!"

Then the van was gone, lost in traffic. Stone was amazed at how much traffic there was.

"Where are the banks on the island?" Stone asked.

"Straight ahead, those that are still standing. You know, that man came in yesterday on a Hawker from Teterboro. It's still on the ramp, and I'll bet that when he cashes his check, or whatever, he'll be heading back to the Hawker."

"Then let's go back to the airport," Stone said. "And thank you!"

The man turned on his lights and spun the car around.

"No lights," Stone said, and he switched them off.

"Sorry about that," the driver said.

Traffic was still heavy, but the driver took a couple of shortcuts to get them back sooner, and shortly, they were driving onto the ramp. "There's the Hawker taxiing," the driver said.

"Take us to the Gulfstream, there," Stone

said, pointing. He called Faith on her phone.

"Yes?"

"Start engines, we're following the Hawker."

Stone gave the driver another hundred, and they hit the ground running. Soon they were taxiing, and the Hawker had taken off.

"He came from Teterboro," Stone said to Faith. "He could be going back there."

"He can clear customs there, or he can stop at an official arrivals airport on the way back, like Fort Pierce."

"Do the best you can to follow him."

"I've got his tail number on my traffic screen," Faith said. "So we'll know what he decides. Also, we're likely to be on the same frequencies, so we may be able to hear his radio calls." She took off and followed the Hawker. "He's calling Miami Center. He's been cleared direct to Richmond, which is where the Jaike Three arrival procedure starts for Teterboro." She requested the same.

Stone had flown that arrival dozens of times; it lined up traffic and kept separation until a landing clearance had been issued, usually for runway six.

"You may as well go relax," Faith said. "We've got three hours or more to go."

Stone went back into the cabin and

flopped into a seat next to Dino.

"I think we're going to bag him," he said. "Can you arrange a reception committee?"

"I believe I can manage that," Dino said, and reached again for the satphone.

52

Stone was snoozing, when he felt the landing gear go down. He got up, walked forward, and sank into the jump seat. "He's landing?"

"He was; he just asked the tower for a go-around and vectors to Newburgh."

"Where the old Air Force base is?"

"Yes, and the Citation Service Center. They own Hawker these days."

Stone thought for a moment. "Ask for VFR to Oxford, Connecticut. OXC, lowest available altitude."

Faith pressed the button. "Got it, direct and six thousand feet."

"Ten miles out of Oxford ask for a change of destination for Newburgh."

"They'll want a reason."

"Tell them we need a part from the Citation Center."

"That should work."

Stone could see the Hudson River coming

up now. "What's the active runway?"

"We're lined up for it," she said. "I see the Hawker. It's taxiing from the terminal."

That gave Stone pause. "Did you see anyone get on?"

"No, but there were a couple of people on the ramp. I couldn't see which way they went."

Stone made a decision. "Land, and request a rental car from the FBO soonest." He saw a red Ford van driving away from the Citation Center, then lost it as a building got in the way. They touched down and rolled to a stop. "Get some fuel," Stone said to Faith, then opened the door, waved at Dino and Herbie, and ran down the stairs.

The three of them burst out of the building and into the car park, looking for their rental. It was a Volvo station wagon, and they were moving immediately.

"The interstate is that way," Dino said, pointing.

"I don't think he's heading for the interstate," Stone replied.

"So we're working your hunches now?"

"You don't need to come to Newburgh to find an interstate. He has another reason to land here."

Shortly, they were in downtown Newburgh, and Herbie spotted the van.

"Red Ford, half a mile ahead, turning left."

"Got it," Stone said.

"Where the hell is he going?" Dino asked.

"Maybe he has a country house up here on the river?" Stone posited. They were soon in a residential neighborhood, then the van turned into a parking lot and stopped.

Dino read the sign aloud: "Luxury Dog Resort and Spa."

"He's picking up Trixie," Stone said.

"What the hell are you talking about?"

"Frances's Jack Russell terrier. At least, I think that's what he is. A brown ball of fur." They were parked across the road.

"Let's bust him on his way out," Stone said.

"Negative," Dino said. "Sig will shoot it out, and I want at least a SWAT team, and that's going to take time up here."

"And we've got only one weapon among the three of us."

"And half a magazine of ammo," Dino said, "four rounds. If he's got a six-shooter, we're outgunned. And we're surrounded by civilian houses."

"That's a pessimistic way to look at it," Stone said.

"I don't know another way, given the circumstances. I think we need the state police, not the locals." Dino got out his cell phone and started punching numbers.

A dog and owner were leaving the building about every minute. "Check-out time," Herbie said.

"Or maybe the yoga class ran over," Stone replied. Then Sig followed Trixie out of the building. Trixie made three pit stops on the way to the van, and Sig waited patiently.

"He's moving," Stone said.

"Don't press him," Dino said. "I don't want a backwoods car chase in a strange neighborhood."

"Admit it. You don't think I could keep up."

"That, too," Dino said.

"He's not going back to the airport," Stone said. "At least, not the way we came."

The van hugged the river, headed south.

"You think he's alone in the van?" Dino asked.

"Except for Trixie," Stone replied.

They drove for another half hour, with Stone keeping three or four cars between them. Herbie had his cell phone out. "He's headed for the Palisades Interstate Parkway, is my best bet."

"Then the George Washington Bridge," Stone said. "We could trap him there."

"I'm not shutting down that bridge at rush hour," Dino said. "I'd have to find a job in another state."

"How about the other side of the bridge, when he turns down the Henry Hudson Parkway toward the city."

"That's a great idea, unless he goes in the opposite direction," Dino said.

"I told you, I'm working hunches. I think he feels safer in Manhattan."

"Weirdly, I agree with you," Dino said.

Sure enough, Sig turned south. After five minutes or so, traffic came to a halt on the West Side Highway. Nothing abnormal about that. Slowly, the traffic began to inch forward until, ten minutes later, they came to a red van, parked sideways in the middle lane, while the other cars picked their way around it.

"I hope he had a heart attack," Dino said. He jumped out of the car, ran to the rear door of the van, and yanked it open, then he ran back to the Volvo and got in. "He bailed," Dino said, pointing at the greenery beside the road. "Now he's just another dog walker in Riverside Park."

Dino blocked traffic while Stone drove around the van, then they were running south for the next exit, at Seventy-ninth Street. After the exit they came to a roundabout which allowed an exit or returned one to the highway. Without slowing around, Stone drove entirely around the circle.

"Hey!" Dino said, annoyed.

"He's not in the park," Stone said.

"And you know that, how?" Dino asked.

"Hunch," they said in unison.

Stone got out of the car and walked a few steps to the main pontoon of the Seventy-ninth Street Boat Basin. He gazed out over the river and saw half a dozen or more small boats making their way up- or downstream.

"Hunch?" Dino asked.

Stone said nothing, just looked up and down the river.

"I'm all out of hunches," he said, eventually.

53

Dino dropped Stone off at his house, then took Herbie and himself away. Everybody slept in his own bed that night. Nobody knew where Sig slept.

Stone's phone rang early. He picked it up and spoke, "We didn't search the marina."

"My thought exactly," Dino replied.

"It came to me about ten seconds before you called."

"I've already ordered a search of all the boats," Dino said. "Give 'em another couple of hours. There were at least forty boats there, and that's forty cold entries and searches. I hope to God he's not there. We'll look like fools."

"I'm not a cop," Stone said. "You may reserve that pleasure for yourself."

"That's very kind of you," Dino said. "Oh, somebody just handed me a piece of paper: two motorcycles were stolen in Soho last night."

"Okay, no foot search of Manhattan."

"I could just give orders to shoot any male driving a motorcycle," Dino said. "We could get lucky."

"Save your luck for something that won't send you to prison," Stone said.

"Let's take a day off," Dino said.

"How do you know Sig is taking the day off? There are still people on the hit list he has promised to murder, myself among them."

"We need to do something he won't expect," Dino said.

"We could do that, if he expected something and we knew what it was."

"I'm just sayin'."

"A meaningless turn of phrase. Don't feel you have to talk just to fill the air with noise."

"Are you telling me to shut up?"

"Yes, until you have an actionable idea."

"Your actionable idea took us to two countries yesterday."

"Three, if you count this one. And we had sight of him in each of them. That's a pretty good score for hunches, isn't it?"

"It would be a fantastic score, if we had scored."

"Well, I for one am entirely willing to cede the search to your thousands of policemen

335

and anybody else who cares."

"Dinner tonight, Clarke's?"

"Seven," Stone said, then hung up.

Stone decided to turn the day into Sunday. On Sundays, he read the *New York Times* cover to cover and watched the political shows on TV. He had to settle for the daily *Times,* but the political shows were all recorded, and Holly Barker was on two of them. He had forgotten that the presidential election was being held the following Tuesday, and although Holly was ahead in most of the polls, she was ahead only by a point or two.

His phone rang. "Hello?"

"Don't worry," she said, "it's not Dino."

"I'm so glad, baby. How are you?"

"I'd be a lot better if I were a lot further ahead in the polls," she said.

"Where are you?"

"The pollsters are calling it a statistical tie, and I'm scheduled to be on MSNBC in four minutes, so I'd better be at Rockefeller Center."

"So near, and yet so far away," Stone muttered. "Any chance you could shake loose for a tryst?"

"My team warns me about every ten minutes that seeing you between now and

Tuesday could have catastrophic results."

"They know you that well, do they?"

"They believe they know *you* that well. I'm not positive, but my chief of staff may have ordered the Secret Service to shoot you on sight."

"They'd enjoy that, wouldn't they."

"They'd rather arrest you and get their picture taken hauling you off to jail in shackles."

"I don't think I'll leave the house until next Tuesday," he replied.

"Good thinking. You can watch me on television."

"I don't suppose you can get naked on television?"

"Good guess. I'm not allowed to speak the words 'naked' or 'sex.' They are not to pass my lips."

"I'm very sorry to hear that."

"You may not talk affectionately to me on the phone, either. My staff is absolutely positive that any phone I can reach is tapped."

"By whom?"

"The Russians, maybe. They would love to torpedo me."

"That's one way to put it."

"Oh, I almost forgot. A pass to the election-night party is being delivered to you. Don't lose it."

"In Washington?"

"In New York. The committee has taken the whole of the Carlyle Hotel, every room, bar, nightclub, and dining room. After three PM, nobody can enter the hotel without the little pass."

"What color is it?"

"The standard is blue, but there are silver, gold, and platinum ones, as well. Yours is the latter, so afterward you can have it melted down and turned into a tie pin, or something. Also, it opens the door to two rooms: a bedroom across the hall from my suite and my suite. You're welcome anytime, after the polls close, when your presence can no longer do any damage."

"And what time is that?"

"Nine o'clock in New York."

"And when do I have to leave?"

"If I lose, never."

"And if you win?"

"Ask me in eight years — less, if they can think of a reason to impeach me."

"I'm torn," Stone said. "I wouldn't want to see you impeached, but . . ."

"What?" Somebody was talking to her. "Gotta run. I'll see you on TV." She hung up.

Stone switched on the TV with a couple

of minutes to go. He wondered if he'd still be allowed to attend the election-night party, if Sig were still on the loose.

The music came up, and a freshly barbered Chuck appeared on screen and introduced the Democratic candidate for President of the United States.

Stone thought Holly looked sunny, composed, and absolutely smashing in a tailored suit and long pants. There must be someone following her around with a brush and comb, he thought, because her hair was absolutely perfect — glowing, even. He settled back to watch and almost immediately dozed off. When he awoke, Holly had been replaced by a panel of journalists who argued about her chances.

54

Dino picked him up on schedule, and they were driving up Third Avenue when Stone suddenly yelled, "Stop!!!" The driver slammed on the brakes and the big SUV skidded to a halt.

"What the hell!" Dino shouted.

"Look at that!" Stone said, pointing at a brightly lit showroom.

"At a store window?"

"At what's in the window."

"A motorbike?"

"It's not a motorbike. It's a 1951 Norton. I've wanted one all my life."

"But you know nothing about motorcycles," Dino pointed out.

"The hell I don't!" Stone snorted. "Before I met you I rode one to work every day, but it was only a Honda 180."

"You're not making any sense," Dino said.

"Wait here, I'll be right back."

Stone went to the shop's door, but it was

locked. A lone woman was seated at a desk across the room. He tapped his signet ring on the glass, and she drew a finger across her throat. *Closed,* she mouthed.

Stone dug out his police badge and held it so she could see it. She got up, approached the door, and peered at the badge.

"Police!" Stone said helpfully.

She unlocked the door, but the chain was still on. "What do you want?" she asked.

"I want that motorcycle," Stone said, "if the price is right."

"The price is not right — not for a cop's wallet, anyway."

"Let's have a look at it up close."

"You're sure you're a cop?"

"See that man in the back seat of the SUV with the light on top?"

"Yes."

"Ask that man. He's the police commissioner of New York City."

She waved at Dino and beckoned him over. He got out of the car and approached. "I've got a crazy person here who says you're the police commissioner," she said. "Anything to that?"

"Well," Dino said. "He's crazy, but he's not lying."

"Lemme see some ID."

Dino pulled back his coat to reveal his

badge and his piece.

"Oh, all right," she said, unlocking the chain, "but believe me, you can't afford it."

"I'll be the judge of that," Stone said, stepping into the showroom and approaching the bike reverently. He reached out to stroke the metal.

"Ahh!" she said. "No touching."

"I can buy it only if it's real," Stone said.

"Okay, one finger."

Stone stroked the gas tank with one finger. "How much?"

"I told you, you can't afford it."

Stone whipped out his cell phone and did a search on Norton prices. "Says here seventeen thousand five hundred dollars."

"In your dreams," she said.

"All right tell me *your* dream."

"My boss's dream is twenty-five grand."

"Call your boss and tell him you've got an offer for twenty grand, cash, right now."

Doubtfully, she got out her phone and pressed a number. "Harvey, I've got a cash offer for twenty grand for the Norton in the window." She listened for a moment, then covered the phone. "Harvey says twenty-five grand, cash, and it's yours. I warn you, don't lowball him, or he'll hang up."

"I'd like to speak to him."

"Harv," she said into the phone, "I think

a personal appearance is required." She hung up. "He'll be right out. Maybe."

"Maybe?"

"If he's in the mood."

"Sold at twenty-five thousand dollars," Stone said. "And I'll need a full tank of gas, the original owner's manual, and the factory tool kit." He saw a display of helmets on the wall. "And the best helmet you've got."

She spoke to her boss. "He wants to speak to you," she said, hanging up the phone.

A door at the rear of the showroom opened and a small man wearing greasy coveralls entered.

"I am Stone Barrington," he said. "I just bought your Norton."

"Have you got twenty-five grand cash on you?"

"I've got that between my checkbook and credit cards."

"I'll need all cash, right now. I've got a buyer at twenty who said he couldn't get the cash until nine o'clock tonight."

"Hang on," Stone said. "Dino, how much cash you got on you?"

Dino whipped out his wallet and counted. "Two grand," he said.

Stone turned back to the owner. "My friend, the police commissioner, and I have four grand between us. I'll give you a check for the rest."

"The police commissioner my ass," Harvey said. "You think I'm going to fall for that?"

"Harvey," the girl said. "He really is the police commissioner. I saw his badge."

"Mr. Barrington," Harvey said, "I'll give you half an hour to come up with the cash."

"Done," Stone said. He turned to the woman: "Tell him what's included." He got out his phone and called Joan.

"Yes, boss?"

"Joan, I need twenty-five grand in cash right now."

"Which court?"

"I don't need bail, I'm in a motorcycle shop on Third Avenue, almost at P.J.'s."

"The one with the Norton in the window?"

"That's the one."

"I was hoping you wouldn't see it. I'll be there in ten minutes." Stone hung up and turned to the owner again. "Harvey, the cash will be here in ten minutes. While I'm waiting, I'd like to see the title, the original title, the registration, and the original owner's manual — and the original tool kit. Oh, and I'd like it filled up and your best helmet and delivered to my house in Manhattan tomorrow morning at ten."

"Doable, as soon as I see cash," Harvey replied firmly.

"Let me speak to Gilly," he said, turning to the woman.

"You shouldn't have told him my name, Harvey. He's creepy."

"I am not creepy, I'm an attorney-at-law."

"Yeah? A minute ago you told me you were a cop."

"Used to be. Retired."

"You really want to do this, Harvey? Okay." She went to her desk, unlocked a drawer, and came out with a fat envelope and a soft leather case.

Stone pulled up a chair, shook out the contents of the envelope, and went through the paperwork. To his astonishment, it was all there. A little greasy, but there.

Then, two people entered the showroom — Joan, through the front door, carrying a bank bag, and a young man, through a rear door, carrying a five-gallon jerry can. They all met in the middle, and money changed hands. Joan left. Harvey signed the title and offered his hand. "All yours, Barrington."

Stone shook the hand. "Was there really another buyer?"

"You bet your ass there was, but he's late with the money, and I don't do late."

"What did the guy look like?"

"Six-two, wiry, beak of a nose, name of Sig."

"Harvey," Stone said, "I'm going to ask a favor of you."

"You can ask," Harvey replied.

"When Sig shows up, I want you to tell him that the bike has been sold, but the new owner is at Clarke's, and he might deal. Tell him the guy's name is Frank, and he's having dinner at Clarke's, across the street."

Harvey looked worried. "I don't know if I want to break that news to Sig. He looks like he knows how to handle himself."

At that moment, a cell phone rang, and Harvey fished it out of a pocket. "This is Harvey. Oh, hi, Sig. No, I won't wait until tomorrow. In fact, I just sold it to a guy named Frank, who's eating a steak at Clarke's, across the street, as we speak. You could talk to him. He says he'll deal." Harvey hung up to cut off the sputtering noises coming from the phone. "He's all yours, Barrington. I'm getting out of here. You, too, babe."

Stone gave Harvey his card, with his address for the delivery tomorrow morning. "Call first and tell my secretary, Joan, exactly what time you're arriving. She'll

346

open the garage door. Have you got a vehicle that will hold it?"

"I've got a trailer."

"Back into the garage, unload, and leave."

"You got it," Harvey said. He poured gasoline into the tank and with a wave, locked them out of the shop. He was last seen pushing the Norton into the back room, followed by the woman.

"See you tomorrow, Harvey," Stone called after them. "Let's go," he said to Dino, "I'm hungry."

"We'll need another chair at our table," Dino said, "since you've invited Sig."

55

They were settled at their table at P. J. Clarke's when Stone asked, "Did you reload?"

Dino stared at him. "Why?"

"You had only four rounds the last time we talked about this."

"I reloaded: I've got a full magazine in the weapon, one in the chamber and two loaded magazines in my shoulder holster. You?"

"Same here."

"Why are we worrying about this?" Dino asked.

"Well, I just want to know we can handle him if he walks in here and starts shooting."

"Why would he do that? He doesn't know where we are."

"Dino, didn't you hear me tell the motorcycle guy to tell him we're at Clarke's?"

"Shit, I forgot about that. Why did you do that?"

"I couldn't think of any other way to find him."

"Then we'd better get out of here, before he shows up," Dino said, hipping across the seats and standing.

"What about our steaks?" Stone asked.

"If he comes, how long will he take to get here?"

"He must be in the neighborhood. He found the Norton."

Dino flagged down a waiter. "Keep our steaks warm," he said, and headed for the back door. "Come on, Stone, we can't have a gunfight at Clarke's."

They hurried out the back door and into the street, which turned out to be deserted.

"Nothing," Dino said.

"He could be along any minute."

"While our steaks either get cold or over-cooked. How long should we give him?"

Stone looked down the street to the motorcycle showroom, and checked to be sure the Norton was no longer in the window. "Shouldn't take him long," Stone said. Then he perked up his ears. From down Third Avenue, seemingly from the far distance, came a howl. "Not long at all," he said.

Dino heard it, too. "He just shifted gears. We need a defensive position."

Stone looked across the street and saw a construction dumpster. "There."

"Inside a dumpster? This is a good suit."

"Behind the dumpster," Stone said. "Come on." He ran across the street, slammed the open lid of the dumpster shut, and stood behind it. "Okay, now we've got two sheets of steel between us and him, plus whatever's in the dumpster."

"I don't think we can do better," Dino said. "Careful we don't put rounds through Clarke's windows."

The distant motorcycle was only a block away now, and shifting down. The machine, with a single rider, appeared, hopped up onto the curb outside Clarke's, and the driver got off and peered through the window.

"Not yet," Dino said, "wait until he's got the brick wall behind him."

"Is it enough?"

"It's a very old building; they built with two stacks of bricks in those days — no brick veneer."

The man surveyed the interior of the bar for another moment, then began walking toward the rear entrance.

"Hey, Sig!" Stone shouted. "Freeze! Show us your hands!"

Sig went for something inside his jacket

350

and snapped off two quick rounds in the direction of the voice; Stone heard them strike the dumpster with a hollow thump. Stone returned the volley with two shots of his own, but Sig had reversed course and was now in front of the bar window again.

He leapt into the air and landed on the motorcycle; a push of a button brought it to life.

"Not yet!" Dino called. "The window."

Then Sig moved away from the window, but not into the street. He drove up the sidewalk, while Stone and Dino poured rounds into the parked cars lined up in the gutter. In what seemed like a moment, he was turning down Second Avenue and could be heard accelerating.

"Shit!" Dino yelled. "Why did you do that?"

"Do what?" Stone asked.

"Yell at him to freeze!"

"Because I wasn't looking to murder him. I gave him a chance to drop the weapon."

"Yeah, and look what he did instead!" Dino yelled at him. "When you want to kill a guy, you don't warn him — Don't you know that?"

"Oh, you just shoot him in the head?"

"Yeah, and if you'd done that this would all be over," Dino said.

351

"Well, I guess you've got a point," Stone said, "but if there'd been a witness in a doorway or something you'd be doing time for it."

"Me?"

"Yeah, you would have just shot him, and a witness could have sent you away for a long time."

"Tell you what, Stone," Dino said. "Next time we get near him, give me the first shot and keep your mouth shut. I'll deal with whatever a witness might say."

"As you wish," Stone said. "I'll come visit you in Dannemora now and then."

"Now," Dino said, "I think we'd better get out of here, because someone has already called 911, and I don't want to have to explain how all these cars got shot up."

"Let's go see how our steaks are doing," Stone said, and they crossed the street and went into Clarke's through the back door. The steaks were on their table, under lids, but they were still fairly hot.

Their waiter came over. "Hey, Dino, did you catch the gunfire outside?"

"What gunfire?" Dino asked innocently.

"Never mind," the waiter replied, then went away.

Stone dug into his lukewarm steak. "It was a BMW, wasn't it?"

"What? Sig's motorcycle?"

"Yes. A black BMW?"

"Maybe."

"You're a big help. And Sig was dressed in all-black leather and a helmet, right?"

"I think so."

"Then add those things to his description."

"How do you know he won't change everything?"

"I think he really loves the BMW, just from the way he rode it, and I think he thinks he looks really cool in black."

"If you say so," Dino replied. He made the call.

56

Stone walked into his bedroom and found a note on his bedside table. Joan must have left it for him.

Stone,
It's been more than fun, a lot more, but I need to go back to work. I've missed the bakery, missed the people, and most of all, the smell of baking bread. I'm going to spend a lot more time here.
Also, I think it's time for you and me to take a break, maybe a permanent one. I think we've wrung all we can out of each other, especially in bed, so we should just give it a rest. I am very fond of you, though, and who knows how I'll feel in, say, a year?

Your friendly baker

He had been half expecting something like

that, and there it was. In addition to some regret, he also felt some relief. After all, Holly was due in town in a few days, and who knew where that was going? The very least he could do was to be available for her and whatever she wanted.

He stripped off and fell into bed, exhausted. The act of firing a weapon at another human being had drained him of adrenaline. He was pondering, as he drifted off, what Dino had said to him.

The following morning Stone went down to his desk and found a heavy, ivory-colored envelope waiting for him. Inside was the promised ticket, heavily laminated and with a photo ID on the backside. He consigned it to his safe for the time being.

Joan knocked and came in. "It's in the garage," she said.

He had forgotten about the Norton. She placed a helmet on his desk. "They left this, too, and this." She placed a folded one-piece rider's suit next to the helmet, along with the owner's manual and a bill of sale, certifying that the machine had been repaired with genuine Norton replacement parts. He shook out the suit and held it up to himself.

"That works," Joan said.

Stone got into the suit, which fit very well, and walked into the garage. There it was, on its kickstand, gleaming, better than new. There was a pair of gloves in the suit pocket, and he put them on, slipped his cell phone into a breast pocket, then set the helmet on his head and adjusted the chinstrap.

The keys were in an envelope taped to the tank, and he pocketed one and inserted the other in the ignition. Following what Harvey had shown him, he kicked the starter once, and it came to life. He rehearsed the gear-change sequence while still on the kickstand, then he got off and pressed the button beside the garage door. He mounted the bike, pushed off the stand, shifted into first, and motored slowly into the street, flipping down the helmet visor. The garage door closed behind him.

He drove the cycle gingerly across the East Side to the Sixty-third Street entrance to the FDR Drive, practicing shifts, and leaning into the corners as much as he dared. Sweet! At last, he turned onto the highway and, for the first time, really accelerated. He headed downtown, brazenly weaving through the traffic, then crossed the Brooklyn Bridge and got off at the first turn and drove to where the River Café was. Too early for lunch, though.

He reversed course and drove all the way to Harlem before leaving the highway and starting down Second Avenue. By now, the machine was practically an extension of his body, and he drove with more confidence than was probably good for him. He eventually turned onto his street, stopped at the garage door and, having no remote control, phoned Joan.

"I'm outside," he said. "Buzz me in."

"Buzz yourself in," she said. "It's taped to your handlebars."

He found the remote, drove inside, parked the cycle, shut it down, and stroked it like a pet. "You are a very good girl," he said to it, then he got out of his riding suit and went back to his desk.

Joan buzzed him. "Holly on one," she said.

Stone punched the button. "Hello, there!"

"A motorcycle? Really? At your age?"

"How did you . . ."

"Joan told me, of course. This is terrible. Now you're going to drive the thing through a plate-glass window somewhere, and I'm going to have to break cover and visit you in the hospital, and we're going to become a de facto couple, and you'll be dogged by the media everywhere you go, and I'll have to explain why you're driving a motorcycle at your very advanced age."

"I'm not that . . ."

"Yes, you are, you just won't admit it."

"I just drove it to Brooklyn and back, and it behaved beautifully! Me, too."

"I don't want to hear about it. I'll have nightmares!"

"Let's make a pact," he said. "Let's never mention the motorcycle again."

"I can't do that! I'd explode. Besides, what would I give you a hard time about?"

"Okay, how about just until the election. If you win, I'll retire the motorcycle, and you won't have to worry."

She sighed. "That's the best deal I'm going to get, isn't it?"

"Maybe not, but it's the best deal on the motorcycle you're going to get."

"Okay. Did you get your invitation for Tuesday night?"

"I did, and I'm very grateful for the access."

"We're going to have this period between when the polls close and when, maybe, the media will announce that I've won, and during that period I'm going to fuck your brains out," she said.

"Promise?"

"I vow it, because if I win, it will be our last time until I'm a free civilian again and can do whatever I want."

"I've got news for you, kiddo," he said, "you're going to do whatever you want, anyway, and to hell with the media. As long as we don't do it in the street, they'll never lay a glove on you, because Americans want their president to have a sex life, one that they can fantasize about, and you're going to give them that, with all the help from me that I can muster."

She giggled. "And we know how much that is, don't we?"

"That said, I support your suggestion that we have those hours and minutes to be wanton, while you're still, technically, a non-president. And I look forward to every minute of it.

"Set your watch," Stone said. "I'll see you at the stroke of nine o'clock on Tuesday, in your suite."

"Dinner will be waiting, then me," she said. She made a big smooching noise and hung up.

57

Stone called Dino.

"Bacchetti."

"It's Stone."

"I thought you'd be in bed all day after the adrenaline dump."

"Speak for yourself. I was up at my usual hour, feeling great."

"Yeah, sure."

"Anything wrong with me was cured by my first ride on the Norton."

"Already? Have you insured the thing yet?"

"I self-insure."

"Liability insurance is cheap, and you're bound to get sued by somebody, if you keep riding it in the city."

"You have a point," Stone admitted, if reluctantly. "I'll call Arthur Steele."

"What, you call the chairman of the board about motorcycle insurance. Is that just to piss him off?"

"You have another point," Stone said. "I'll get Joan to do it."

"As long as you don't let her ride it."

"Can you imagine Joan on a motorcycle? In one of her tweed suits?"

"Just barely. Don't leave the keys lying around, though."

"You have another point. You're scoring well today."

"I score well every day. You just don't pay attention."

"Has there been any flak about the cars we shot up last night?"

"Of course there has, but we're handling the claims as usual. I did tell them to prioritize cars parked on that block."

"I hope there weren't any Lamborghinis or Ferraris among them."

"We can hope," Dino said.

"Did you get your tickets to Holly's election-night bash at the Carlyle?"

"Yeah. We'll be there. Where's the action?"

"Everywhere. They've booked the whole hotel."

"I bet I know where your action will be."

"If you do, avoid it. We'll be busy."

Dino gave a coarse laugh. "You'll be high and dry for women after that," he said.

"Don't count on it. Shouldn't a single president be able to have a sex life?"

361

"Okay by me," Dino said, "as long as she runs the shop right."

"Holly is not a lazy person. You needn't worry about that."

"Viv gets back this afternoon. Dinner tonight?"

"Patroon? Seven-thirty?"

"Done." Dino hung up.

Stone buzzed Joan.

"Yes, boss?"

"I'm going to need liability insurance on the motorcycle."

"How much?"

"Ten million."

"Not nearly enough. If you get sued, the plaintiff will go for the moon, once his lawyer figures out who you are. A good lawyer would tell you to register it under a corporate name. And I'd go for fifty million."

"You think Arthur will go for that?"

"I'll take care of it with his secretary. He'll never know."

"Okay, negotiate."

"Consider it done, and don't ask any questions. I won't tell you what the premium is."

"Oh, all right, go!"

"Oh, I forgot to tell you: your bike's license plate arrived this morning."

"You mean I went riding all over town without a plate?"

"You went riding all over town?"

"Sort of."

"I'll put the plate on. Pretend it's always been there." She hung up.

No sooner had she gone than Stone's cell rang. "Yeah?"

"It's Dino." He didn't sound happy.

"What's wrong?"

"Sig did another name on the list late last night."

"Who?"

"What does it matter? You don't know any of them. It would have been after we saw him."

"Well, that pretty much ruins my day."

"Don't let it. It's not your fault."

"You keep saying that. Why don't I believe you?"

"You just enjoy feeling guilty," Dino said.

"I'm hanging up now," Stone said.

"Listen to me. Go armed."

"Got it." Stone hung up. Upon further consideration he retrieved his little Terry Tussey .45 auto and its light shoulder holster and hung it next to his jacket.

At a little after seven, Stone's phone rang: in-house call.

"Yes?"

"It's Fred, sir. If you're going out for dinner this evening I'd let me drive you; rain coming."

"All right, I'll meet you in the garage at seven-fifteen." He hung up, got out his iPhone and went to Weather Bug. Radar showed heavy rain west of the city.

It was drizzling when Stone arrived at the restaurant, and as he left the car, Fred handed him an umbrella. "You'll need this when you return to the car. There's no awning."

Stone went inside, checked the umbrella, and joined the Bacchettis in their usual booth. "You're looking wonderful," Stone said to Viv. "Travel somehow improves you."

"You're a very convincing liar," she said, returning his kiss. "You must get a lot of practice."

"Calumny!" Stone retorted. "Learn to accept a compliment!"

"Yes, sir," she said, and drinks arrived on the table.

"Rain tonight," Dino said.

"So I hear. It was only sprinkling when I arrived, but Fred insisted on driving me and gave me an umbrella, too."

"Fred is a smart guy. Listen to him."

"Is the rain going to affect something you're running tonight?" Stone asked.

"Probably. I've got every motorcycle we own on the streets looking for that black BMW you identified."

"Did I mention that every BMW motorcycle I've ever seen was black?"

"Now you tell me," Dino said, picking up his phone and passing that information to his men.

58

It was raining lightly, but steadily, as Stone got into the Bentley, and he was grateful for the umbrealla Fred had given him.

"Home, sir?"

"Yes, Fred. You were right about the rain."

"The National Weather Service is rarely wrong," Fred replied. Ten minutes later, they drove into the garage.

Stone went upstairs, undressed, and got into a nightshirt, then he propped himself up in his electric bed and tried to find a station with no news of Holly, which was making him more and more anxious as Election Day approached. He settled for an old movie he loved, but he didn't get far into it before he dozed off.

He was awakened by his cell phone, charging beside him; the clock read 3:05 AM. "Hello," he said hoarsely.

"You're in bed already?" Dino asked.

"Most people are at three in the morning."

"Hear that?"

"What?"

"Just listen."

Stone took the phone away from his ear and listened. Rain was hammering his roof.

"Okay, I hear it. Anything else?"

"We've got a sighting of our boy and his BMW," Dino said.

"Where?"

"Harlem, 125th Street, driving aimlessly, but so far, he has eluded my people."

"That's just great," Stone said. "Call me back when he's in custody."

"I thought you might like to cruise uptown and join the hunt. There's not much traffic in this weather, except for my guys on bikes and our boy Sig."

"So, you noticed the weather?"

"What's the matter? Do Nortons dissolve in the rain?"

Stone swung his feet out of bed. "Oh, all right."

"Have you still got a handheld police radio?"

"Somewhere."

Dino gave him a channel number. "That's reserved for our motorcycles tonight. Keep in touch."

Stone found the radio buried deep in his dressing room, on a charger. He got into his old motorcycle leathers, which still fit, he noted, grabbed some boots, a slicker, the radio and a light headset with microphone, and his .45 shoulder holster, then dressed and hurried down to the garage. He started the bike, and when he raised the garage door, he was surprised at how much rain was falling. He snapped on the helmet and pulled the slicker over it and drew it tight, to keep the rain from running down his neck. Then he tuned the radio and eased onto the street. The sound of the rain on the helmet caused him to up the radio's volume, and he began to hear idle chatter from the cops who were out. He turned up Third Avenue and was greeted with a nearly empty boulevard, with green lights running uptown. He hurried to catch the sequence and was soon doing forty as the lights stayed green. The wind against his faceplate kept it fairly free of rain, so visibility was good.

When he got uptown there was more traffic on 125th Street, so he had to drive more carefully and wipe the rain off his face guard more frequently. He looked into some side streets and found cars still parked outside Rao's, a tiny Italian restaurant on East 114th Street with a huge following. Stone had been on a waiting list for a table for years, but with no luck yet. There were only ten tables. Occasionally he would get a call saying there had been a cancellation, and he'd take it when he could get it.

He stopped outside Rao's for a minute to stretch, and two police motorcycles drove up, one on each side of him. One of the drivers pushed back his own face guard. "License, registration, and insurance," he said.

"Why?" Stone asked. "You're looking for a BMW, and this is a Norton."

"What's a Norton?" the cop asked.

"A British bike that's older than you are."

"Are you Barrington?"

"That's right."

"We got word that you might be around. Are you on the radio?"

"I am."

"We'll get back to it, then," the cop said, revving his bike. "You'll hear about it, if we spot him."

Stone put his bike on its stand and walked over to the Rao's entrance and stood under the awning, just to get away from the noise of the rain. He took off his helmet and wiped his face.

The door next to him opened, and a voice said, "Stone, is that you?"

"Hi."

"Why are you all dressed up like Evel Knievel?"

"New bike. Just seeing how it goes in the rain."

"Are you out of your fucking mind?"

"Could be."

"Come on in. The help's just sitting down to supper. We'll feed you."

Stone joined the big table and had a meatball and some pasta. The restaurant was famous for its meatballs. He kept the earphones on.

"What's with the headset?"

"There's a cop op on for tonight. I'm listening in."

"What for?"

"You've read about the hit-list killings?"

"Yeah, sure."

"That guy."

"You mean he's around here?"

"Could be. Last spotted in Harlem."

He got up, walked to the front door, locked it, then came back. "That's better," he said.

They all continued eating. Stone declined the wine.

"What's the matter?" he asked. "You don't like the wine?"

"I'm sure it's great, but it doesn't mix with

370

motorcycles on a rainy night." As if to underline his statement, a new wave arrived and drowned out conversation for a couple of minutes, then passed on.

Stone heard voices on his headset and pressed a cup to his ear to hear better. ". . . Harlem, heading downtown . . . Avenue."

"You're going to have to excuse me," Stone said, standing and zipping everything up.

"Gotcha."

"The food was wonderful, as always. When am I going to get a table?"

"When a few people die."

"I figured." He went outside and got on the motorcycle.

59

Stone pulled on his helmet, kicked the engine to life, then turned up the volume on his radio. The hammering of rain on his helmet let up for a bit, and he had better reception here.

"Turning downtown, Second Avenue," a young man's voice said. "Black BMW, rider wearing black."

"Did you get a shot at him?" another voice asked.

"No ID on the guy, but he fits the description. I'm not going to shoot some citizen."

Good boy, Stone thought, being a civilian himself.

"There's another civilian out here on a bike, a Norton, whatever that is. He's a friend of somebody. Don't shoot him, either."

Stone felt better immediately. He shifted gears and got moving. From 125th Street, he swung south on Fifth Avenue, thinking to get ahead of Sig, unspotted. Farther downtown he made a left and headed for Second Avenue. As he turned right again he saw that there was more traffic than before; he was seeing delivery trucks now, some moving and some parked. He slowed down enough in his turn to hear the familiar howl of the BMW, sounding a few blocks away, then he accelerated, ignoring traffic signals when they turned red, but watching carefully for crosstown traffic.

Blocks ahead he saw flashing lights, then the rain came again obliterating his view. He instinctively slowed, and in so doing, passed behind a truck crossing Second in the sixties. He had not seen the vehicle until he was behind it. He took some deep breaths to calm himself, then got his speed up as the wave of rain passed. The flashing lights farther downtown were no longer there. Then, dead ahead, he saw a motorcycle down in the middle of the street, an inert form lying yards south of it. He slammed on his breaks, stopped, and got off. The man was lying on his back, and Stone felt for a pulse at his neck. Nothing. He unzipped the man's jacket and listened at his chest. Still nothing.

Stone pressed the talk button on his radio.

"Mayday, mayday, mayday," he said.

"Who's that?"

"Barrington. Cop down on Second Avenue at Sixty-first Street, no pulse at chest or neck, request ambulance."

"On the way. Cause of death?"

"No visible wounds; maybe an accident. I'll stay with him until . . ." He heard a siren from uptown and looked to see the flashing lights approaching. He waved his arms, then pointed out the fallen cop. Without further conversation, he leapt on his Norton and headed south again, watching side streets. He heard the howl of the BMW again and was trying to get a fix on it when a black machine roared up to him from behind. He didn't have time to react, and the rider swung his fist at Stone's upper body. Only it wasn't just a fist. Stone saw the blade too late, then felt the searing pain and warm liquid running down his arm.

He swung wide of the BMW, then swung back, and braked slightly, aiming his front wheel at the other bike's rear wheel.

Stone braked hard as the BMW went down and slid on the wet street. By the time it was stopped, so was Stone. He dropped his bike where it stood, took off his right glove and stuffed it into his sleeve, hoping to stanch the flow of blood.

The other rider was up on one elbow now, and Stone had his little Tussey .45 in his right hand. He walked over to the rider and kicked him hard in the head, hard enough that his helmet came off. "Good evening, Sig," Stone said and aimed another kick at him.

Sig dodged, and Stone spun around and hit the pavement, and the .45 left him. Sig was on his feet now, and had a switchblade in his hand. "Good evening, Barrington. You've got less than a minute before you bleed to death, but I think I'll cut your throat for good measure." He took a step or two toward him.

Stone was groping for the little pistol, but it wasn't there, and he couldn't take his eyes off Sig, who was still coming. He aimed a kick at the man's crotch and connected, then he scrambled to his knees and looked for the .45.

"Shit!" Sig yelled. Apparently, he didn't enjoy pain.

Stone saw the gun and dove for it. Sig was struggling toward him by now.

Stone knee-walked toward Sig; the gun lay between them. He got a hand on it as Sig drew back to swing his knife again. Stone had no memory of pulling the trigger, but he remembered the noise. He

375

remembered one other thing, saying, "Mayday, two men down . . ." Then he fainted.

Stone half woke in the rear of an ambulance and saw a thick wad of bandages on his left arm and an IV in that vein. He fainted again.

Stone slowly came to in a dimly lit place, where there were monitor screens and beeping noises.

"He's back," a woman's voice said. "Mr. Barrington, can you speak?"

"I don't think so," Stone said.

"That was speech," Dino's voice said. "Take it as a yes."

"Okay," Stone muttered.

Dino positioned himself in Stone's line of sight. "I've got two pieces of good news," he said.

"Give me the good news first," Stone said.

"You now, officially, have Italian blood."

"Huh?"

"I know that, because it's my blood. They ran short, so I gave them a pint."

"An order of garlic bread, please," Stone said.

"You want the other good news now?"

"Okay."

"Sig is missing nearly half of his head. That little .45 of yours removed it."

"Yeah, but is he dead?" Stone asked.

"No, he's down the hall, giving a tap-dancing performance," Dino replied.

"Then go shoot him again," Stone said, then he felt like a nap.

60

Stone was kept for two nights in the hospital. Finally, after an inspection by two surgeons and the application of a sturdy bandage, his nurse sat him up in bed and carefully got his arm into a sling. "It has to stay this way for a while," she said, "to keep it from further damage, so don't get too frisky. A nurse will come around every morning to inspect the wound and change the bandage." She gave him his cell phone back. "It's been off since you arrived, so you probably have a few messages."

He checked, and he had some, but none from Holly.

Dino drove him home and deposited him outside, where Joan waited to walk him in. "Have you spoken to Holly?" Stone asked before he got out.

"Yes, and she knows where you've been."

Joan helped him out of the car. "I'm sure

you'll want to go right back to work," she said, archly.

"What I'd like is to go straight to my own bed," he replied.

He woke up in time for a hot supper served in bed by Helene. Still no word from Holly.

The following day a nurse turned up, liked the look of his wound, and bound it again.

"Do I still have to keep it in the sling?" he asked.

"A few more days."

He made it a point to move around the house and not walk like a cripple.

By Election Day he felt normal, but the nurse still insisted on the sling. Fred took him to his local polling place, where he voted for Holly, then came home.

"What are you doing for dinner?" Joan asked.

"I'm dining at the Carlyle at nine," he said, retrieving his pass from the safe."

Joan handed him a gift box from Hermès. "Open this before you go."

As evening came on he shaved, showered, and slowly dressed in his tuxedo. He seemed to have lost some weight, so he wore his red suspenders to keep his trousers in place. He had to take off the sling to get into his shirt, and he couldn't reach high enough with his left hand to tie the bow, so he had to call Joan upstairs to do it for him.

She helped him into his waistcoat, then wound his Patek Philippe pocket watch, set and installed it, with its gold chain, in the waistcoat. She got him into his jacket and inspected him. "Good," she said.

"I'll need my sling."

She opened the Hermès box to reveal a beautiful black-and-white silk sling, which she tied and hung around his neck. "There," she said.

"Glorious!" He pecked her on the cheek.

"Do you ever wear that evening cape you had made?" she asked.

"Not once."

"This might be a good night for the debut. You'll look less like an invalid."

"Good point."

She draped the cape, which fell to just above his knees, around his shoulders and hooked the silken rope closure.

"Go get 'em. Fred is waiting for you at the curb; you don't have to sneak in and out of the house anymore." She hung his platinum pass around his neck, too. "So they won't throw you out."

Stone took the elevator downstairs and

outside, where Fred was waiting with the Bentley. They drove up Madison Avenue and made the turn onto Seventy-sixth Street, then stopped at the side entrance to the Carlyle. He got out, went through the revolving doors, and entered the lobby, which was filled with people wearing pass cards around their necks.

A Secret Service agent frisked him with a wand. "She's in 27 A," he whispered to Stone.

"Thank you." He walked to the elevator, where he was looked over again by other security men, then got into the elevator.

"Good evening, Mr. Barrington," the operator said. "Twenty-seven?"

"Thank you, yes."

The elevator sped upward and disgorged him on the twenty-seventh floor, where two Secret Service agents stood on either side of the door to Suite A. They knew him, so didn't bother to frisk, then one opened the door for him. Holly stood before him in an emerald-green gown that set off her red hair, looking like a star from Hollywood's golden years. She came toward him, arms out, then stopped. "Which arm?" she asked.

"The left," he replied.

She reached for his right arm and placed her other hand on his cheek and kissed him.

"Good evening," she said.

"Can you help me out of this cape?" he asked.

She unhooked the closure and swept it away. "Beautiful sling," she said.

"Joan supplied that."

She led him to the sofa and sat him down in front of a glass of Knob Creek, then she sat down beside him and picked up a phone. "I don't want to be disturbed until all four networks have called it," she said, then hung up.

"How are you feeling?" Stone asked.

"Strangely calm, yet nervous," she said, picking up her martini and taking a sip. "I expect to be calmer still after this goes down. Dinner is in fifteen minutes."

They dined close to the windows, with the view of Manhattan to the south spread out before them. She cut his meat for him. They chatted like the old friends they were.

"How are Ham and Ginnie?" Stone asked of her father and his girl.

"Wonderful. They'll join us later in the evening." She sighed deeply. "I'm so glad this election is over. It's been exhilarating, but exhausting."

"I can imagine," he said.

"No, you can't. You would have to live

through it."

They demolished a large part of a porter-house steak, with béarnaise sauce, new potatoes, and haricots verts, followed by crème brûlée. They ate slowly and it was after eleven by the time they moved to the sofa for a glass of port.

As they sat down, the phone rang. Holly set down her glass and picked up the receiver. "Yes?" She listened for a moment, and the expression on her face changed from neutral to pained. "Thank you," she said, and set down the phone. She convulsed once, and tears spilled down her cheeks.

"I'm sorry," Stone said.

She gasped, drawing in a deep breath, and made a visible effort to calm herself. "The polls were wrong. I won forty-one states, an estimated sixty-seven percent of the vote."

Stone smiled and raised his glass. "Madam President," he said.

They watched the pandemonium on television until nearly midnight, then she changed into something more presidential-elect and went down to the ballroom for Kate to speak to her country and the world.

END
November 5, 2019
Key West, Florida

AUTHOR'S NOTE

I am happy to hear from readers, but you should know that if you write to me in care of my publisher, three to six months will pass before I receive your letter, and when it finally arrives it will be one among many, and I will not be able to reply.

However, if you have access to the Internet, you may visit my website at www.stuart woods.com, where there is a button for sending me e-mail. So far, I have been able to reply to all my e-mail, and I will continue to try to do so.

If you send me an e-mail and do not receive a reply, it is probably because you are among an alarming number of people who have entered their e-mail address incorrectly in their mail software. I have many of my replies returned as undeliverable.

Remember: e-mail, reply; snail mail, no reply.

When you e-mail, please do not send attachments, as I never open these. They can take twenty minutes to download, and they often contain viruses.

Please do not place me on your mailing lists for funny stories, prayers, political causes, charitable fund-raising, petitions, or sentimental claptrap. I get enough of that from people I already know. Generally speaking, when I get e-mail addressed to a large number of people, I immediately delete it without reading it.

Please do not send me your ideas for a book, as I have a policy of writing only what I myself invent. If you send me story ideas, I will immediately delete them without reading them. If you have a good idea for a book, write it yourself, but I will not be able to advise you on how to get it published. Buy a copy of *Writer's Market* at any bookstore; that will tell you how.

Anyone with a request concerning events or appearances may e-mail it to me or send it to: Publicity Department, Penguin Publishing Group, 1745 Broadway, New York, NY 10019.

Those ambitious folk who wish to buy film, dramatic, or television rights to my books should contact Matthew Snyder, Creative Artists Agency, 2000 Avenue of the Stars, Los Angeles, CA 90067.

Those who wish to make offers for rights of a literary nature should contact Anne Sibbald, Janklow & Nesbit, 285 Madison Ave, 21st Floor, New York, NY 10017. (Note: This is not an invitation for you to send her your manuscript or to solicit her to be your agent.)

If you want to know if I will be signing books in your city, please visit my website, www.stuartwoods.com, where the tour schedule will be published a month or so in advance. If you wish me to do a book signing in your locality, ask your favorite bookseller to contact his Penguin representative or the Penguin publicity department with the request.

If you find typographical or editorial errors in my book and feel an irresistible urge to tell someone, please write to Sara Minnich at Penguin's address above. Do not e-mail your discoveries to me, as I will already have learned about them from others.

A list of my published works appears on my website. All the novels are still in print in paperback and can be found at or ordered from any bookstore. If you wish to obtain hardcover copies of earlier novels or of the two nonfiction books, a good used-book store or one of the online bookstores can help you find them. Otherwise, you will have to go to a great many garage sales.

ABOUT THE AUTHOR

Stuart Woods is the author of more than eighty novels, including the #1 *New York Times* bestselling Stone Barrington series. He is a native of Georgia and began his writing career in the advertising industry. *Chiefs,* his debut in 1981, won the Edgar Award. An avid sailor and pilot, Woods lives in Florida, Maine, and New Mexico.

The employees of Thorndike Press hope you have enjoyed this Large Print book. All our Thorndike, Wheeler, and Kennebec Large Print titles are designed for easy reading, and all our books are made to last. Other Thorndike Press Large Print books are available at your library, through selected bookstores, or directly from us.

For information about titles, please call:

(800) 223-1244

or visit our website at:

gale.com/thorndike

To share your comments, please write:

Publisher
Thorndike Press
10 Water St., Suite 310
Waterville, ME 04901